Team Mom

Team Mom

Franklin White

www.urbanbooks.net

Urban Books, LLC
97 N18th Street
Wyandanch, NY 11798

Team Mom Copyright © 2014 Franklin White

ISBN 13: 978-1-60162-409-3
ISBN 10: 1-60162-409-3

First Trade Paperback Printing May 2014
Printed in the United States of America

10 9 8 7 6 5 4 3 2 1

*This is a work of fiction. Any references or similarities
to actual events, real people, living or dead, or to real
locales are intended to give the novel a sense of reality.
Any similarity in other names, characters, places, and
incidents is entirely coincidental.*

Distributed by Kensington Publishing Corp.
Submit Wholesale Orders to:
Kensington Publishing Corp.
C/O Penguin Group (USA) Inc.
Attention: Order Processing
405 Murray Hill Parkway
East Rutherford, NJ 07073-2316
Phone: 1-800-526-0275
Fax: 1-800-227-9604

Team Mom

by

Franklin White

1

Coach set his cleats firmly into the warm Bermuda turf on the football field to watch his new team run laps around the track. So far, there was not one player on his middle school park team who he could automatically point to and declare a stud. He'd done it many times before, even considered himself an expert at evaluating a player who would lead his team. Not this time, though. Under his breath he looked out at his prospects and declared, "No pop. No swag. No good right now." Maybe if he made them run faster, he could find what he was looking for. He yelled out, "C'mon, guys. Pick it up a little. Can't you lift your feet off the ground any higher than that?"

Just at that moment a woman approached him from behind. She was black and petite, with a real snazzy short haircut like Halle Berry's. She had on a white silk blouse and a black skirt and didn't mind standing on the turf with her high heels on. "Excuse me. Are you the coach for the middle school team?" she asked.

Coach turned around. He was multitasking now, still looking for that special player and answering her question at the same time. "Yes, yes, I am." He extended his hand. He gave her a quick glance, then looked back at the team. "Rob Madison, but everybody calls me Coach."

After she let go of his hand, she said, "Sorry we're late. Busy workday. We got here as soon as we could." She turned away from Coach and fixed her eyes on her son, who was standing at least seven yards behind her. He was on the track that circled the field, in fact. She said, "My son wants to play on the team."

Coach moved his eyes away from the woman, over to her son, then quickly gazed at the team chugging along around the track. "You brought him here to play football?" Coach asked to make sure.

The mother smiled. Just the thought of a child growing into manhood and being able to compete made all parents smile. Coach smiled too, because he completely understood. During all his years of coaching it wasn't out of the ordinary for a mother to bring her son out to practice and to introduce him. Coach wasn't judging, but this particular mom looked a little younger than most with a teenage son.

Coach looked over at him. "Why are you standing back there? Come here and introduce yourself."

The woman turned around quick to face her son with tightened eyes upon hearing Coach's instructions, wavering on whether or not she wanted to backpedal like a defensive back and grab his ear, then drag him over to where they stood. He was about four inches taller than his mom in her heels, but she could probably do it, anyway. "Get over here, Jarques." Her words and tone were sharp. "I don't know why you're standing way back there, anyway," she told him.

Coach watched him as he hesitated and then slowly strolled over with his head down. Coach didn't like his body language. Coach watched some of the players make their way past him on the track for another lap. He still hadn't found what he was looking for and let them know they needed to pick up the pace before he walked over to Jarques.

Jarques saw him coming and dropped his head an inch or two more.

"Get your head up. How can I see your eyes when you're looking down at the ground?" Coach wanted to know.

"What did I tell you about that?" his mother said.

Coach sized him up. He was lean, had long arms, and looked to be close to 175 pounds and six feet tall. Coach had read somewhere that Deion Sanders had the same type of build in high school but was not as heavy. He even looked a bit like Prime Time. "You're a nice size," Coach said to him. "So you want to play football for the Panthers, huh?" Coach now had his hands on his hips and looked his new prospect up and down.

The young man nodded his head yes, and his mother kind of stomped her heels on the turf and put her hands on her hips in disapproval.

"What position?" Coach said.

"Quarterback," he whispered.

"Quarterbacks talk louder than that, young man."

Coach reached out to shake his hand. The teen reached out, and when he finally got up the nerve to shake the coach's hand, his handshake was as weak as his body language. Coach felt the pressure of his handshake and tightened his own grip and moved in closer to him.

"Handshakes are firm." Coach squeezed some more. "You got that?"

2

Fuck me, was the pounding thought in Coach's mind. It was the next day, and he was on his nine-to-five public relations stint for the police department. Days like this made him wish he coached football full-time. All the time. He was in a meeting with a group of community citizens and two home-owners' associations. Initially, it was supposed to be a meeting of only five or six people, tops, but things had changed. When he arrived at the overflow room of the church, where the meeting was being held, at least two hundred people were in attendance. Within two minutes after he gave his spiel about the police department's commitment to safety to the residents it served, it was time for the worst part of it all, which was opening up the floor for questioning.

There was a man sitting in the front row, on the edge of his seat. He'd been frozen in the same position since the start of the meeting. He raised his hand, indicating he had a question. "What the hell makes these young boys do the things they are doing out here in these streets? I'm seventy-two years old, and the only reason in my life that I want my youth back is to knock one of these assholes out." He didn't even pause for some of the reaction and laughter in the room. "I have a nice house. I've been there for over fifty years, and I'm not leaving until they put me in the ground. So what makes them think they can just rummage through my mail, take my retirement and Social Security checks?"

"I'm sorry to hear you are going through that, sir," Coach said to him.

The man replied, "Sorry? I want your department to come out and make some arrests and bust some heads. These guys aren't hard to find. All they do is walk around the neighborhood all day, deciding on what house to break into."

Coach was also becoming increasingly fed up with the inability of his department to control the break-ins. But he remained the ultimate company man and was well versed in giving the politically correct answer to community members who had requested to speak with the police department. He said, "We have upgraded our patrols, but honestly, sir, there is only so much we can do. I spoke with the commander in the district, and he promised me he would put a stop to all the break-ins in your area. But until then, I would suggest everyone keep an eye out for one another, and when you see anyone suspicious in your neighborhood, call police immediately."

There was another man in the first row who looked to be in his sixties. He was more reserved. Seemed to be exhausted by this meeting and maybe how life was going in general. Or he needed some coffee or a boost from that energy in a bottle or something. His expression had remained the same throughout the meeting. He said, "Yeah, yeah . . . we all know the drill, but that doesn't stop the break-ins. In my estimation, the mayor needs to push for more jobs for these young folks. In my day we had jobs and didn't have a need to take someone else's belongings by breaking into houses all damn day long."

The lady sitting next to him stood. She wasn't one of the seniors. She could have been in her forties but looked no older than thirty-three. The outfit she was wearing told everyone she wished she was twenty-one. She had on tight jeans, pumps, and a Lady Vamp T-shirt with more than a few bangles around her wrists. You could hear the bangles every time she moved her arms. "There used to be respect too. Where's our respect?" she said. "When I go out for a walk or ride my bike, it never fails that one of those Lil Wayne or Young Jeezy look-alikes approaches me with the most ignorant talk you'd ever want to hear. I'm a grown woman, and I'm afraid to even imagine what they are screaming out to our younger ladies trying to get back and forth to school."

The questioning went on and on for another hour, and Coach didn't have a legit, soothing answer they wanted to hear. He couldn't tell them more cops would be on the streets soon, wouldn't tell them the crimes would stop. He dared not say the police force had a plan to find those responsible and prosecute them to the fullest extent of the law. Because they were right. The community had become a freaking milieu of dark days filled with frequent occurrences of the unthinkable: murders, rapes, abductions, shootings, baby killings by babies themselves because they were forced to watch siblings at an age when they were not equipped as their parents were out chasing a rap career or some shit.

At one point during the conversation he wished he was back on the detective squad, locking up the bastards who were causing the commotion. But in the back of his mind, he knew why going back there was out of the question. All the violence and black-on-black crime had gotten the best of him. Right now, at this moment in his life, he was interested in the community and somehow making it better. Somehow.

"I know things aren't looking good on so many levels," he told those in attendance. "But let me share something with you that is a good thing." He was facing stone-faced souls now. And it was quiet as hell now too. He cleared his throat, then said, "Well, it's my football team."

"Football team?" a woman repeated. It was almost an echo.

He looked in her direction. "Yes, right here in our own community, and we've just started practice for our upcoming season."

"What's that got to do with us? We can't play," the same woman's voice rang out. She chuckled at her own question. Then there was some chatter about bad knees, cardio trouble, allergies, and a whole bunch of other shit that sedentary folk had.

He told her, "It's a chance to show your support. I coach these boys and talk with them every day, and one thing I've noticed in the time we have been together is they don't have enough support," Madison informed them.

"That's their parents' job," someone mentioned.

That comment caught Coach's attention. He almost got a case of the ass but laughed the comment off. "Really? Well, I remember my father telling me that back in the good days . . . Y'all remember the good days, don't you?"

Someone mentioned Marvin Gaye, and then someone else said that those were the days of love. Then another person started talking about trust and true friends and family. The comments were followed by some amens.

Coach noticed he had finally connected with them, and he was damned if he was going to let it go. "I remember when communities supported their sports teams. I think that if some of the kids playing were supported by those in the community, it would create a more family-like atmosphere around here."

A few people started to heckle, taking Coach by surprise, because that quick after reeling them in, he was fucking losing them. He overheard someone say they had shit to do right in the basement of the church. He looked out toward the middle of the room.

"Hey, I live in this community too. I want it to be better," he told them. The heckling stopped. "I do," he told them again.

"I don't know. . . . These kids have no respect for anything, and their parents need to start first, not us," said a lady in a red hat.

Coach was not getting anywhere with this group. They had been worn down by the conditions and the actions of the youth and no action by the police department. They wanted to live their lives in peace without the obligation to give back. The Black Panthers and the civil rights era were long gone, and even if those at the meeting had benefited, they wanted no part of the new digitalized generation. Coach could understand it but did not get it completely, because these kids needed them, whether they realized it or not.

A man standing in the back raised his hand. He was black and had an all-gray beard that was trimmed to perfection. When Coach acknowledged him, the man pressed his hat to his chest after straightening out his overcoat. The first time he tried to speak, his words didn't seem to come.

He cleared his throat and tried again. "I used to play football," he said. "Played at Capital University in Ohio before I moved down here. Played with the great Albert White in nineteen sixty-two and all those boys who won all those games and were drafted into the NFL, all the while going to a little ole Division Three school and getting a degree in business. I tell you, those were the days." He pointed toward Coach, who was standing at the front of the room. "But I think he might have something there. When I played, the entire community would come out and support us. We would see them in the streets, and it was like we were old friends, just because of that funny-shaped ball."

It was quiet for a beat as Coach let the man's words soak in.

The man pointed at Coach with his hat. "So what do you need us to do?" he asked.

Coach smiled and jumped at the opportunity. "Nothing, nothing at all, other than come to our first game. I'll even make sure we have a few police vans come out and pick you up and take you to the game free of charge."

It became quiet again.

"We're not going to be in the back of those vans, are we? I ain't never been in the back of a police van, and I'm not going to start now," a man called out, breaking the silence.

Amid the laughter that filled the room, Coach said, "No, no, these are the best we have. They're just like buses."

3

Coach was exhausted, but in the end, he felt encouraged by the meeting. At least he'd recruited some fans for his team. He stayed until every last person left the overflow room in the basement of the church. The meeting had sparked a reminder to go see an old friend, to call on him for help with the team. He and the team were going to need all the help they could get. On the way out to his car, he stopped when he heard his name being called by a female voice.

"Hey, Coach," the woman said. She had a wondering smile on her face.

"Hey," he said back. He actually had to focus to get his bearings. After a beat or two he remembered who she was and said, "Oh, hey. J's mom, right?"

She smiled again and said, "And before I forget, let me thank you for calling Jarques . . . J. He has really taken to his nickname, and it seems to have put a hair or two on his chest."

"Oh, yeah?"

"Yes, it has," she said. She looked at him, very curious. She was focused on his police uniform. "I know it's really hectic out in the streets, chasing these crazy criminals and all . . . but what are you doing here? Laying it all down at the altar before you hit the streets or something? Getting that special covering?" She pointed at his police uniform.

He looked down at his uniform. Then he straightened out his tie. He got her point and placed a smile on his face. He chuckled too. "Oh, no. I just finished up with a community meeting. I'm done with the streets. I'm doing public relations for the department nowadays."

"Oh, what kind of meeting y'all have up in here?" she asked.

"Community meeting, letting everyone know the streets are safe and hearing some concerns they have about protection and all the break-ins that have been occurring."

There was kind of an awkward silence now. She appeared to be holding back her thoughts on crime in the community and how well the police were doing. She'd just heard on her car radio about a young teenager who was kidnapped from her home.

"But one good thing came out the meeting," he continued.

She smiled again. She had just swallowed her thoughts about crime. "Yeah? What's that?"

"Recruited some fans for our first game."

"Fans?"

"Sure did. Right at this meeting. It should be fun," he said. There was another awkward moment, and he looked into the church, then back at her. "So I guess it's my turn to ask. . . . What're you doing here? Getting ready to ask the Lord to forgive your sins down at the altar?"

He chuckled, and she smiled.

She said, "Good idea, but probably too late for me. I work here."

"Really?"

Her tone was point-blank and not very happy. "Really."

"Not the best, huh?"

"It's okay," she replied, as if trying to make herself believe it. Then she lowered her voice and added, "Actually, this fuckin' place gets on my last nerve." She looked around again. "But we do what we have to."

Coach was trying to read the woman, who had just cursed in front of the church, without judging her. All he could do was chuckle at her instincts. "Yeah, you are right about that," Coach cosigned. He looked back at the church, then nodded to a few people who had been in the meeting with him who were walking past and wished them well.

"So I guess I will see you and J at practice tomorrow."

"Okay. Yeah, sure," she agreed.

Coach started to walk away in the direction of his car. He stopped and looked back when she called out his name.

She said, "I got the flyer for volunteer positions on the team. Put me down for team mom."

He was taken aback, so much so that he even sat his briefcase on the ground. "Team mom?"

She said, "Dang . . . Why so surprised?" Her face displayed amazement. Then she gave him a smile.

Coach was amused at that moment. "Not surprised. Stunned a bit, though."

"Why is that?"

"Because I usually have to beg someone to take the position."

"Not me. I can handle it, so put me down as team mom, okay?"

"Okay. Thanks. It's done. I'll introduce you at the next practice."

"Good. See you then," she said. She started on her way.

Coach picked up his briefcase and turned around to leave, but then he twirled around and called out to her. "Wait a minute. I forgot your name."

She smiled. "It's Shonda. My name is Shonda Black."

4

Luckily for Coach, it was Wednesday, which meant no practice. There was one place he needed to be besides that church to save his soul, and it was front and center at his favorite sportsbar. The plan was to meet his longtime friend Calvin Wilson to talk some shop, get a meal, and drink plenty of ice-cold beer.

"You want me to do what?" Calvin wanted to hear what Coach was asking one more time. This was right after Coach hit him with an unexpected request. Calvin was so surprised at his request that he stood up from his chair at the table, and that was when anyone looking could see he was about five-ten and had an athletic build. Just like a running back.

"Calvin, this is serious. I need you to help me coach my team," Coach repeated.

Calvin looked at the near-empty pitcher of brew and began pouring it in his glass, then changed his mind. "Fuck it," he said. And instead he lifted the pitcher to his mouth and gulped the beer straight down without a care. He pointed to himself with the pitcher. "Me coach? Oh, hell no. I'm done with coaching, man." Even though there was music and televisions on throughout the establishment, Calvin was pretty loud and at that moment could be heard by a few of the early birds filtering in to get their drink on.

Coach said, "Look, Calvin, you have to let that go, man. Just let it go."

For some reason Calvin hadn't cleared his mind of the situation that had his name rolling in mud in the community. The situation was still playing loudly in his mind, and one thing these two guys agreed on and always wanted to make sure of was that their names stayed out of any kind of scandal while they coached ball. They truly looked at coaching as their community service.

Calvin still had the pitcher in his hand. "What do we have to do to get some more of this?" He looked around. By this time he was a few seconds from going over to the bar himself to ask the bartender for another if their waitress didn't arrive soon enough.

At the moment Coach wasn't too engaged in his efforts to get more brew. He had a huge appetite and was paying more attention to what was on his plate: a baked potato, baked chicken, and a salad.

Calvin looked over at his meal, still holding the empty pitcher, and asked, "After all this time, you still not eatin' red meat?" For Calvin, it was kind of fucking unbelievable. Shit, un-American even.

"Nope," Coach said.

"How long has it been?"

"About as long as you've quit coaching."

"Funny. Two years?"

Coach moved his head up and down. Then he dived into his salad. He put a tomato on his fork before the lettuce. Then some chicken.

Calvin looked at his plate and watched Coach enjoy his meal, then said, "Damn, that's serious. You still eat pussy?"

Coach didn't answer but stared at him longer than it would have taken him to answer with a yes or no.

Calvin said, "Look, man, how long have we known each other?"

"I'm getting ready to say, 'Way too long,' but I would guess and say at least eleven, twelve years," Coach answered.

"Twelve to be exact, and five Georgia Youth championships to show for it," Calvin said.

"And that's exactly why you should come back." Coach still loved his beer and drank some of what he had left in his mug. In an imaginary way he was beating his chest because he got a point in over his friend at Calvin's own admission.

Calvin looked into the empty pitcher of beer and thought about the offer again. "I don't know, man. These kids today don't listen worth anything, and the parents are even worse." He gasped at the site of the empty pitcher and turned it upside down.

"Are you still on that situation, Calvin? Look, that is over with."

The waitress finally came over, grabbed the pitcher, and let them know she would be back. She looked at Calvin kind of oddly too. When Calvin finished looking at her tight little ass walking away in her jeans, he answered, "You talking about that asshole accusing me of texting his wife?"

Coach chuckled a bit. "Yeah, that's it. But it was a little more than texting he accused you of." The situation had Calvin tied in knots.

"Man, I had people coming into my shop, asking me about that. There isn't anything more broke down than a preacher gossiping about something that's not true, even though it involves his wife." He remembered it all too clearly.

"But you handled it. It turned out okay," Coach said.

"Yes, it did. But a preacher took me to a limit where I was going to knock his ass out. Thinking I wanted to do his wife . . . Now, I've done some things in my life."

"Of course. We both have," Coach told him, still eating.

"But that? Me? A preacher's wife? I don't do that, man."

The waitress returned with another pitcher of beer. She poured them some.

Coach didn't let up. He was on a mission. "So, what do you say, Calvin? I have over fifty kids who have been discarded by the middle school system. Can you believe no gotdamned money for football? How the hell does that happen?"

Calvin poured some beer and took a few gulps. "Hell, I don't know. I ain't on that screwy-ass board that makes all the decisions. If it was up to me, they would be playing in the Georgia Dome instead of the Falcons."

Coach said, "They want to play some ball, but I can't coach them all by myself. It was cool when they were younger and I had just enough for an offense and defense, but I have numbers now. I'm talking boys that will be in high school soon."

"Fifty kids, huh?" Calvin sucked down some more beer. Enjoyed it too.

"Or more," Coach replied.

Calvin raised his mug to his mouth and drained it. "What type of offense you running?"

"Pistol. Lots of motion and some read option," Coach informed him. "If I can find me a quarterback."

Calvin poured himself another beer from the pitcher. He smiled. "What the hell, man. You haven't won without me in the last two years, anyway."

5

The team's personnel was finally in place. As promised, Calvin joined the coaching staff, and Coach was grateful to Shonda Black for filling the post of team mom. After several weeks of practice the team took on a rival neighborhood team in a scrimmage and looked better than anyone could expect on the hot summer evening.

Coach and a few stragglers, along with Calvin, were gathering up equipment after the scrimmage and dumping ice water out of coolers. Calvin noticed a few Gatorades left in the cooler, reached down through the chilling ice, and tossed one to Coach, then cracked another open for himself.

"We looked good today," Calvin said.

"Yeah, man, you have that defense on point."

Without any hesitation, Calvin said, "I'm scratching it. I think I want to go with something else."

"What do you mean? We beat them twenty-eight to seven."

"They scored on us, Coach, and that's a problem for me," Calvin told him.

"Shoot, man, when I asked you to come back, I didn't know you had this much fire left."

"Can't lie, I missed it. Missed everything about this."

"Good to see the passion, because you're going to need it tomorrow for the fund-raiser," Coach said.

"Say what?"

"The fund-raiser. The one we've been talking about the past few weeks. We need to get some extra money for the uniforms, team meals, and trophies for the end of the season for all the players. You know how this works, Calvin."

Calvin said, "When have you ever known me to participate in a fund-raiser?"

Coach stood still, thinking about it. "I don't remember."

"Exactly. I don't do fund-raisers. I will put a donation can up at my place of business with a photo of our team and hope someone finds the goodness to leave a little something in the can." Calvin was the owner of a postage stop shop. "But as far as standing on the corner, begging or washing cars, big daddy ain't with that. If I were you, I'd ask the parents for an extra bump. They would probably rather do that than wash a car or barbecue. What are you doing, anyway?"

"Haven't you been listening at the end of practice?"

"Guess not. Maybe my brain shuts down at the sound of the word *fund-raiser*."

"We are doing a barbecue and car wash. The usual. I thought about asking the parents for more money per child, but let's see how this goes."

"Well, let me know too," Calvin replied as he dumped the rest of the ice onto the field.

Coach said, "Whatever. So who'd you like at quarterback? J or that kid Boston?"

Calvin looked up. "I like Boston. He's more physical. Mind seems to be a bit tougher. He can take a lick, get back up, and act like it didn't happen. But that kid J runs around back there too much. Trying to avoid that hit. He's the fastest, though. Damn he's fast. Gotta arm on him too."

"Yes, sir, they both can throw it. So I'm J at this point."

Calvin said, "Practice should tell you a little more about them. I will pin the D's ears back a little next week. You know, go after them, help you make a decision."

"Cool," Coach replied.

6

A sign that said CAR WASH AND BARBECUE was placed high on the back of Coach's truck bed for all to see after he parked his truck front end forward toward the Shines Barbecue Pit, which was allowing the team to use its lot for their fund-raiser. No matter how the media tried to portray Atlanta and its surrounding area as a high-end, fast-moving sector of the country, it would never lose its essence as a place where a good car wash and a fish fry with lemonade could always bring in the cash. Coach and most of the team, along with some parents of the team members, were all well rested and ready to wash cars and give out coupons for a tasty barbecue chicken sandwich at Shines to anyone who supported their efforts. During the lunchtime rush the crowd at the location began to swell, and so did the drama.

A parent approached Coach as he was standing by the grill, showing two of his running backs how to turn the meat on the grill. Coach took it upon himself to educate his players in any area he could, and they were listening too.

The parent asked, "Hey, Coach, do you have a minute?"

Coach sensed by the parent's tone that it was going to be a conversation for his ears only. He walked away from the grill and realized the lady who had approached him was the mother of one of his linemen. She kind of smiled at him. Then she came right out with it.

She said, "I'm sorry this is not what I normally do, but some of the other mothers along with myself feel that the shorts the team mom has on are highly inappropriate."

Coach was taken back because he didn't know Shonda Black was even at the event. Plus, he'd never been put in the position where he would have to look into a grown woman's wardrobe selection and appearance.

Coach pointed at the lady who was speaking to him. "Ms. Thomas, right?" Coach asked, just to make sure.

She smiled and shook her head yes, pleased that Coach remembered her name.

"You're saying she's dressed inappropriately?"

"Uh-huh, that's right. She is dressed like one of those freaky video girls on television, you know, the ones that cause you to scream at your son to shut the television set off."

"Is that right?"

The woman had Coach's full attention, and her eyes were connected to his 100 percent. She said, "I think what she has on . . . Well, she thinks those are shorts. But me and a few of the other moms feel like they are more like panties, see-through at that."

Coach tried to take it all in. Despite his hesitation, he was making an effort to read the mother. He wondered what the hell she wanted him to do about it. He looked around for the team mom. All he could see were the players still at the grill and some standing out front, near the road, holding up signs letting oncoming traffic know about their fund-raiser.

"Oh, she's in the back, helping with the cars," the woman informed him. "We'd really appreciate it if you talked to her. Maybe ask her to change into something less revealing. Christ, cover up at least. I mean, everything seems to be just hanging out. . . . I'm just saying."

There was a pause, followed by a brief stare down. On the surface Coach thought this was pure bullshit. If he were back on the streets in a squad car and got a call like this, he would hop back in his car and drive off without thinking twice.

Conceding, he said, "I'll look into it."

She smiled, then walked away, looking back at Coach twice before she went back to her team mom lookout position.

Coach didn't want to rush over to where the cars were being washed. It would give the appearance that he was automatically siding with the women who had a complaint. He wasn't sure if there had already been words between any of the women. Just in case, he went back to the grill for about ten minutes before he went to see what the commotion was about. After all, they were just shorts.

The ten minutes went by entirely too fast. Before Coach made his way over to check on the shorts, he took a drumstick off the grill, then went into the cooler for a grape soda. Then, with caution, he walked to the back where the cars were being washed to see what the fuss was all about. He was surprised at who he saw all up in the mix.

"Calvin?"

"The one and only. What's up, bruh?" Calvin had soap suds on his hands.

Coach said, "You tell me. Thought you didn't do fundraisers?"

"I do when I get calls that tell me that I need to check out the view." Calvin had a wide grin on his face. He pushed his head in the direction of a car that was being washed. When Coach looked over, all he could see was the team mom whirling and twirling in soap suds while washing a car. She was helping a few players who were attempting to get the hood of an SUV squeaky clean. "Nice, right . . . ?" Calvin noted.

Coach tried not to stare, but the team mom, Shonda Black, was just standing there, devoid of even the slightest bit of concern. Coach didn't realize it, but he was staring. It was more a longer look-see than a glance. He was trying to put things in perspective perhaps and decide if she was out of line or not.

"Nice . . . right?" Calvin said again. Then he nudged Coach on his arm. "Damn. Why are you staring like that? I can't take you anywhere, Coach."

Coach said, "What do you think about what she's wearing? Borderline, right?"

"Nah, not one bit," Calvin confirmed. "Not one bit at all."

She had on shorts, a tight-fitting tee, and flip-flops. There was no doubt she spent time in the gym.

When Shonda Black, the team mom, bent down to retrieve the water hose, it seemed as though the entire lot became quiet. But it could have just been Coach's imagination messing with him.

"Did you hear that?" Calvin wanted to know.

"What?" Coach asked.

"That silence when she bent down. Or was it just me?"

Coach had to ponder his initial thought, then dismiss it and clear his mind. "Calvin, please, man. She's grown, right?"

Calvin hadn't taken his eyes off her. "Sure is . . ."

"Shorts and a T-shirt, man. That's all it is. No foul, no harm." Coach announced, having decided the outfit passed inspection.

"I don't know about all that, because she is hurting me," Calvin said. "But what I do know is you need to have more of these fund-raisers."

Coach looked around to assess the situation again. The first person he saw was none other than Ms. Thomas. She was standing with her arms tucked tightly over her big breasts, waiting to see what he was going to do about Shonda Black. Three other mothers had their eyes peeled too. Coach read the ladies and scanned the crowd just like he did during his nine-to-five. At first he thought about going over to speak with the team mom, maybe pulling her aside. But that wasn't a good idea. He didn't know her like that, and maybe she would get pissed. He decided to walk away instead. He could see Ms. Thomas turn her hands up skyward, then drop them down to her sides. Coach could hear Calvin ask him where he was going, but he kept walking away.

Coach had never been the type to loud talk his players, even when others thought he should. He would speak directly to them. He preferred the one-on-one approach. He'd always been a stickler for respect. Getting it and giving it. It was going to be the same way when he spoke with the team mom. Unbelievably, with everything else going on, he was now on booty patrol. Coach knew her son, J, was out front, directing drivers into the car wash, so he walked over to him and asked him to go get his mother because he needed to speak with her.

When she finally made her way over to him, her T-shirt was soaked and her nipples were trying to escape from her shirt. She took a deep breath before she spoke. "Hey, Coach. What's up? This turnout is wonderful, isn't it? Who would have guessed I would have so much fun? What's up? You need me to do something for you?"

Coach took a deep breath and blew it out. "Hey . . . Shonda."

She forced her eyes tight, wondering why Coach was hesitating and shit. Then he said her name again. She waited for him to speak.

Coach said, "Shonda . . ."

She confirmed that her name was, indeed, Shonda. "Yes, Coach, that's my name . . . Shonda Black."

"Right. Look, I have to tell you something." Coach was looking into her eyes, but more than once his eyes traveled down to her shirt to her nipples, which were gesturing at him and bidding him hello. For no other reason than respect, he took his sunglasses, which were hanging on his shirt, and put them on. "Okay, I'm going to come right out and say this."

"Okay . . . ," she replied.

"Um, I'm getting a few complaints about what you have on."

She smiled because she was shocked. "What?" She looked at her clothes. "What's wrong with what I have on?"

"Well, I've had heard some grumbles about the ensemble you're wearing."

She began to laugh, then looked over in the direction of the women in the back, where all the cars were, and then back at Coach. "I knew it. I always go with my gut feeling. You ever do that, Coach? I just knew those ladies were gawking at me."

"Is that right?" Coach asked.

"Yeah, whispering and shit," she sang.

"Seems that . . . I'm not saying who . . . but they don't want their sons seeing all your—" Coach stopped.

"All my what, Coach?"

Coach moved his hand up and down. "All of . . . this . . . all of you . . . well, your shorts and shirt, I guess."

"Well, I hate to break it to them, but those little girls that go to school with their sons dress worse than this. The men of those ladies who are talking about me enjoy seeing a woman in the hot-ass sun, working, not afraid to wear comfortable clothing. Have you seen what some of those mothers have on? All those tired-ass leggings and hot-ass jeans and freakin' polyester shirts up to their necks? Having the nerve to have a weave on . . . standing under umbrellas, sweating their asses off. Shoot, they just jealous, Coach."

Coach was still trying to digest everything she had said at a hundred miles an hour.

"Okay, okay, Shonda. Can you just stay in front with me? Maybe just hold the sign out front or something. I will send the rest of the boys to the back to wash the cars."

She looked at Coach and started to laugh. "Okay. I can do that. I am not trying to be back there with those tired-ass ladies, anyway."

7

The car wash became so packed that afternoon that Coach had to stop letting people in. It was like magic. Shonda Black, in all her sparkle, went out to the street, holding a sign that read SUPPORT OUR TEAM AND WASH YOUR CAR. And within minutes cars were lining up, requesting the deluxe wash for ten dollars. Calvin wasn't too happy, as he had to pitch in and get grimy and wet in the trenches along with the boys. After all was said and done, the team made close to two thousand dollars to cover their expenses.

Afterward, Coach wanted to go to his favorite sports bar and drink some brew with Calvin. But Calvin barely had enough energy to drive home after working so hard during the car wash. All he wanted to do was sleep.

So Coach decided to go alone. He found a nice little quiet spot in the bar. It was in a corner with the perfect view of the big-screen TV. About forty minutes later, after having enjoyed some much-deserved time alone, Coach looked up and found Shonda Black, the team mom, standing at his table, smiling.

She said, "You have to remind me to put your number in my phone."

Coach was confused but smiled at her, anyway. He put down his beer; then he wiped his mouth.

Shonda continued, "That way, I could have called you and let you know I was on my way. I'm still on the staff, right?" She snickered. "You didn't kick me off because of my ensemble at the fund-raiser, did you?"

Coach didn't get a chance to answer her. It was like she was waiting until he opened his mouth to speak to cut him off. Plus, he was still amazed that she was standing in front of him.

"I overheard Calvin tell you he couldn't make it, so I thought I would come by here, to see if you were here."

Her presence made more sense now to Coach.

She pulled out the chair on the other side of the table. "You don't mind, do you?"

Coach laughed a bit. "No, c'mon. Sit."

The moment was sort of awkward for him. Not for Shonda Black, though.

She said, "So, is this what you do? Come to the sports bar, watch football?"

"Yeah, it's what I like to do from time to time."

She looked around, sized up the layout of the sports bar, the people inside, the football banners. There were some baseball ones too. A different sport was on each of the televisions. She took a glance at the poster of Serena Williams, then put her eyes back on Coach. "What do you eat?"

"Depends."

She looked at the pitcher of beer. "So I take it you're just thirsty tonight?"

Coach rested his eyes on the half-done pitcher in front of him. "Guess so."

"So what's your waitress's name?"

Coach wondered what she meant. His eyes told her so.

She repeated her question to Coach, this time really inquiring "What's your waitress's name?"

Coach looked around. "Hell, I don't know."

"You sure?" The way she looked at him, she might as well have asked him one more time.

Coach chuckled a bit. "Yeah, I'm sure. Why?"

"Just sayin'. Coach . . . you're not here with anyone, so I thought just maybe you'd come to see a waitress or something."

Coach needed some more beer to go along with her question. Then he asked her, "What makes you think that?"

"I used to be a waitress."

"Oh, I get it. Quite a few visitors, huh?"

"I had my share," she said. Shonda's eyes cut to the television screen, and she gave Coach a chance to gather himself and take another gulp of his suds. Then she said, "Is that all you're drinking tonight?"

He looked down at his beer mug. Yeah, think so."

"No shots? Are you scared of shots, Coach?"

"Hold up. I never said that."

"No?"

"Hell, no. Shot's don't deter me."

She was laughing now. "Right. You look like a one-and-done type of drinker to me."

"Trust me, I'm not him."

She smiled and taunted him by saying, "Oh, yeah?"

"That's right."

She looked around the sports establishment, smiling the entire time. "I am so glad you got a table way back here in the corner, then," she told him.

"Why is that?"

Shonda said, "This is why." Then she put her hand deep down into her oversize Fendi bag and pulled out a fifth of her favorite tequila, Pepe Lopez, and a packaged shot glass. She pushed them over to Coach and then pulled out a pink shot glass from her bag for herself without another word until they both had two shots each.

8

Lois Gregory, a woman in her early seventies, had just finished dinner in the kitchen of her home. She lived alone and actually enjoyed it. A few times during dinner she heard voices outside her home, and after she put her dishes in the sink, she went to her front door and opened it to look outside. When she peered outside, she noticed a group of young males standing in front of her home. They noticed her, even though she was trying to conceal herself behind the screen door. One of the males, who was wearing jeans with the right pant leg rolled almost all the way up to his knee, decided he was going to be the spokesman for the group.

He said, "Can we help you?" His boys thought his ass was funny.

Lois Gregory told them all, "Get away from here. Didn't I tell you boys, I don't want you around my house?"

All of them laughed and spewed out some disrespectful comments, which she refused to hear.

The male with the rolled-up jeans started to show out and nodded his head up at the screen door. "Like we care what you say. And I am not a boy. I'm a man."

Lois grabbed the front door handle nice and tight in case she needed to shut the door quickly before she said something else, even though her screen door was locked. "A man?"

He said back to her, "You heard right."

At this stage in her life Lois wasn't about to start letting any disrespectful fellow just talk to her any way he wanted. She couldn't exactly tell their ages, but she was going to treat them just the way they were acting. "What are your names? I bet your parents don't even know you're out here," she said.

They looked up at her screen door, and there was a pause before they began to laugh again. The same guy said, "We don't know their names." He pointed to one of his friends, who seemed like he couldn't stop smiling for some reason. "At least he don't." Then he pointed at another dirtbag. "And he don't, and most definitely not him."

Smiley boy said, "Aww, you don't know yours, either, and that's real talk."

"Well, that's the problem, then. Now, get away from my house, before I call the police," Lois said.

The leader of these guys just wouldn't shut up and leave. He said, "The police don't scare me."

Lois said, "Well, they should, because I will have them lock you up."

"Is that right?"

"Yes. Now, get away from my house. You don't even live around here."

Mr. Spokesman stood there for a moment. As he paused, he looked at his boys, then back up at the screen door and Lois. This time he spoke very slowly. "You better watch your mouth, old lady, before I come up there and beat you like they used to back in slavery."

The group laughed and drew together in a circle as a car made its way down the street in their direction.

It was Mr. Tall. He was inside some kind of Buick with two doors. When he noticed the group in his neighbor's yard, he rolled down the window of his car with his hand. He paused a few seconds once the window was all the way down and looked the group up and down right before he gazed up at the door of the house. He couldn't see Lois directly but could tell she was behind the screen door. "Everything okay out here?"

The guy talking all the smack leaned forward and squinted his eyes to see in the car. "Oh, is this the police you were talking about? Old Otis here?" he wondered aloud.

Once again his followers laughed at their fearless leader.

Lois snapped, "Hush your mouth and respect your elders."

"Fuck you, old lady," he said back.

Mr. Tall didn't blink one bit before he spoke. "Okay, you fellows better get out of here before they have to call the meat wagon for you."

The boys laughed again, and it was evident who the leader of this crew was, because his ass wouldn't stop talking. He said, "What you going to do, old man?"

Without letting them know, Mr. Tall moved his hand to the passenger's seat and picked up his pistol and hit the hammer hard. They heard it click.

Mr. Smiley was not as dumb as he looked. He said, "Oh, shit. That's a gun."

"Sure is, and it's pointed directly at your ass," Mr. Tall confirmed.

"Let's go," said the leader. He looked up at Lois as they walked away and growled, "You better watch yourself."

Mr. Tall responded for Lois. "And you should too."

Lois and Mr. Tall watched them fade into the darkness, which was quickly falling.

When she was sure they were gone, Lois opened her screen door and her face appeared. She waited a beat before she spoke.

"Thank you again, Mr. Tall."

"No problem, Lois Gregory. Are you going to be okay?"

"Yes, I'll be okay. If I wasn't so tired, I'd invite you in for a while."

He smiled and said, "If I wasn't so tired, I'd come in too."

They both smiled and just thought about the possibilities of spending time together.

Mr. Tall was firm when he told her, "Lock them doors and keep them locked, okay?"

"Will do," Lois responded, right before she turned around to go back in the house.

He said to her, "If you need anything, I'm right down the street, okay?"

"Like you always are, Mr. Tall. Like you always are."

Mr. Tall looked in the direction in which the young men had walked, waved at Lois, then drove slowly down the street.

9

Coach and Shonda Black sat in the back of that sports bar and had at least four shots apiece with a plate of steamy hot wings and fries. Shonda revealed that she didn't have a ride home, because her girlfriend had dropped her off, and asked Coach for a lift. Even though Coach was taken aback that he was now her ride, because normally after drinks at the bar it was straight home to bed for him, it was cool. He felt good to have such an unexpected great time. Shonda lived only a block away from the football field, so dropping her off wasn't too bad, anyway. Coach had an idea before taking her home. As he drove past the field, they pulled into the parking lot to chat some more.

"Sometimes, I come out here and sit," Coach told her.

She said, "In the dark?"

"Sometimes, yeah."

She looked around in the darkness. Couldn't even see the field. "What's it do for you?"

"I don't know. But it does something, you know, just knowing when I'm out here with the kids, I'm helping on some kind of level, other than locking these young boys up."

"Being on the streets really got to you, didn't it?"

"Can't lie," he admitted. "It was getting hard looking into the eyes of these young men once you throw them in that cell. I don't care what anyone says. If you haven't looked into a young black boy's eyes when he's thrown in jail and haven't realized he's confused, scared, and knows there's a better way but hasn't been taught what that way is, then you are really part of the problem."

"Oh, shit, Coach. You getting deep up in here. You don't mind, do you?" Shonda pulled out the bottle of tequila, cracked it open, and took a swig. "Fuck a shot glass this time."

Coach shook his head and laughed. "Damn, girl."

She had to wait until the burn from the tequila subsided before talking. "What?"

"You are enjoying yourself tonight, aren't you?"

"Told you, I have to. Son's gone to his friends for the weekend and no work tomorrow. I can sleep in as late as I want. Yeah, I'm enjoying myself tonight."

Coach pushed his head back on his headrest. "I ain't mad at you."

Shonda put the cap back on the bottle. "So are you going to get in any trouble being out drinking with the team mom?"

Coach turned to look at her. "What kind of trouble?"

"Uh, I don't know. From a lady who might be at home, waiting on you, perhaps?"

He kind of smiled. "Oh, no. Nothing like that."

Shonda thought about what he had said, then looked over at him. "Are you a player, Coach?"

Her question surprised him. "What?"

"Just trying to find out if you are a player or not. I mean, you're a handsome man. Hard to believe you don't have a woman to go home to. Where's your woman, Coach?" she teased.

Coach looked at Shonda, then back out into the darkness. "Dead. She's dead."

Shonda looked at him. He had her complete attention.

"She died in a car crash about three years ago, along with our twin boys, that she was carrying."

Shonda was still. She wanted to say some kind words to Coach, but they wouldn't come quick enough. The quietness now was eerie and spine-chilling. She didn't know what she should do or say. She just handed him the tequila in the brown paper bag.

Coach looked at her. "Thank you." Then he took a hell of a swig, put the cap back on, and handed the bottle back to her.

"You're welcome," she told him. "You're welcome."

Anyone could imagine that it took a few minutes to get back to the high energy of the night. Shonda felt it was on her since she was the one who was responsible for the break in the action.

"So, Coach, answer this question. . . ."

"Okay . . ."

Shonda had a coy smile on her face. It was too dark to see, though. But the light sarcasm was quite apparent in her tone. "What did you think of my outfit today?" She started to laugh.

Coach was quick. It was as if he wanted to forget about what he had just told her. "I think you pissed some parents off. That's what I think."

"I'm not worrying about those women. Please, they all can be fly too if they hit the gym once in a while. Besides that, how did it look? I mean, did it make *you* *f*eel some type of way?" Coach noticed the brown paper bag with the tequila still in Shonda's hand and grabbed it. "Yeah, can't lie. Everything was in place real nice and tight," he said. "I'm sure your man has his hands full."

Shonda was shocked at his quick jab. "Please! What man? I'm doing me. Have been for the last fourteen out of the twenty-eight years I have been living on this planet."

"Why so? Twenty-eight? Geez."

"One reason is my son. He barely knows his father, and I don't want a lot of men around him like that. That would be wrong on so many levels. I mean, it's not every night I can get away and sit in a truck with a man and drink tequila. But if and when I do get a chance, I like to enjoy myself and have a good conversation and leave it at that, and I'm good. And yes, I'm twenty-eight."

Taking in her words, Coach nodded in agreement.

Out of the blue there was an awkward silence. But the silence had some energy. Energy that they hadn't felt in quite some time.

Shonda spoke first. "You know about being lonely, right?"

"Yeah, I do," Coach said.

"Exactly," Shonda murmured, letting the energy inside the truck say whatever else was on her mind.

Coach understood the energy's message loud and clear. "Exactly," he repeated right before he turned to kiss her.

Shonda reached up and put her arms around his neck and enjoyed the moment of being in the arms of a man. There was no lack of appreciation from Coach.

After a minute or two, Coach backed off. "Whew. Damn, we better go," he said.

Shonda tried to gather herself. "Yeah, it's getting late."

Coach put on his seat belt, pulled out of the parking lot, and drove off.

Shonda ran her hand through her hair and looked up at him. "Where are you going? My place is the other way."

Coach turned on his car radio, and the grown and sexy hit "Come and Talk to Me," by Jodeci, hummed through his speakers. "My place," he said.

10

Things really weren't supposed to end up like this, but Coach and Shonda spent not only Saturday night together but all day Sunday too. They would probably have kept the connection going longer, but motherhood and the daily grind for Coach on the job pushed them apart.

Coach was a mile a minute at work, scheduling meetings he normally hated to attend and answering e-mails with requests that were long overdue. When he felt someone standing over his desk in the squad room, he looked up.

"Don't mind me, son. Keep working, if you have to. I understand it all too well when you get in a groove. Should I come back some other time?"

When Coach's eyes focused on the man standing before him, he couldn't place him. But he was sure he'd seen him someplace before. He just smiled and tried to remember.

"There ain't no need for you to rack your brain trying to remember who my old ass is. I can tell you. My name is Theadore Tall. I met you over there at the church the other day. I spoke up about playing football back in the day, and you invited the community to a game and promised you'd provide transportation in a fancy van."

When Theadore Tall took off his hat and smashed it into his chest, Coach remembered clearly who he was. Coach stood tall and reached out to shake his hand. "Yes, Mr. Tall. What can I do for you?"

Mr. Tall went into his pocket and pulled out a business card. "Well, you gave me this card and told me to come see you if I needed. I came by to tell you that my house was broken into the other day, and I'm wondering what can really go on down here to make these break-ins stop. I don't have much, and I'm okay with that, but what I do have, I would like to keep."

Coach walked from behind his desk. "You weren't injured, were you?"

"Shoot, no. They came in through my back door when I went out to the store."

Coach talked to Mr. Tall for a while and tried to soothe him so that he would feel like he was getting good service from the police department. Coach introduced him to his captain, who set him up with an officer who would take his report about the break-in.

Mr. Tall wasn't too happy about having to sit down and explain in detail that he'd been broken into. But, when he informed them it was the third time in three months, he was told that his home was a priority and was assured that there would be a squad car making its presence known at least once a day. When he finished with the report, he went back out to see Coach at his desk.

"Not too painful?" Coach asked.

Mr. Tall said, "Well, my ass started to hurt in that chair. Other than that, things are fine."

"That's good to know." Coach smiled. "You know, you remind me of my grandfather. No disrespect," he assured him.

"Aww, boy, I'm not sensitive like that. Hell, I know I'm an old man, and I'm glad to be one. Especially today, I'm cool with being on my way out. Wouldn't want to be alive the way this world is headed in ten, twenty years. Nope, not me."

Coach started laughing.

"What? What did I say?" Mr. Tall said.

"My grandfather used to say the same thing."

"Well, how long ago was that?"

Coach thought about it. "About fifteen years ago."

"Um, we'll see. Time is even shorter than I predicted."

"Yeah, I guess so," Coach agreed.

"So, how is that football team going? I hope you know I am taking you up on your kindness. I want to see the first game."

"First game is in two weeks. I will post it down at the church."

"Two weeks?"

"Yes, sir. Boys are chomping at the bit right about now."

"Well, they gotdamn ought to be."

Coach could see the fire in the old man's eyes. "Wow. After all this time you still got passion for the game, That's good, Mr. Tall."

"Let me tell you something."

"What's that, Mr. Tall?" Coach had a fondness for Mr. Tall and was truly interested.

"They used to lock me up in the locker room before the game, right up until kickoff."

"Why is that?" Coach wanted to know.

"Because I couldn't handle my emotions, and I would run into my teammates during the warm-up and knock them the fuck out."

"Yeah, right."

"I'm serious, son. I will have to show you all the write-ups I have. You know, you had to be a bad boy to get in the news in the sixties."

"I guess you did," Coach admitted.

"Ain't no guessing. Back then the only time a black man could get in the paper was when they were stringing his ass up to a tree."

"Look, why don't you come out to practice some time? There's a real nice shade tree where you can sit and watch the action," Coach told him.

"Shade tree?" Mr. Tall questioned.

"Yes, sir."

"Fuck that. I'm wearing my cleats, and I'm working the field with you. What time you coming to pick me up?"

11

After he invited Mr. Tall to practice, there was absolutely no way Coach could keep him away from the practice field. Mr. Tall sat down and spoke with Coach in his office for the next thirty minutes. Before he left, Mr. Tall made certain—damn near made Coach give him his word—that he would pick him up promptly at 4:30 p.m. for practice.

When Calvin arrived at practice, he was taken by surprise by Mr. Tall. "Tell me that is not Fred Sanford on the field," were the first words out of Calvin's mouth when he noticed their visitor.

Coach was placing the blocking dummies and cones and was not paying any attention to the field. "Nope, that's Theadore Tall. He was an all-American at Capital University back in the day, and I invited him out."

"Way back in the day, I bet," Calvin said. "So how'd you meet him? Why'd you invite him?"

"Job related. He's cool man. Listen closely to him and you might learn something."

"Like what? Like how not to wear my old crusty-ass cleats when I'm in my eighties?"

"Calvin, respect him, dude. Plus, I think he's in his seventies. I'm telling you, he's cool. Go introduce yourself."

Five minutes later Coach looked up from setting up for practice, and he could see Mr. Tall showing Calvin and about three early players on the field the correct way to hold the football. Coach was seconds from blowing his whistle to start practice.

"Hello, Coach," said a voice behind him.

Coach looked behind him and saw Shonda Black walking toward him, smiling, and of course, he smiled back.

"How are you, Coach?" she asked.

"I'm good, and you?"

"I'm good too," she said. "You know what?"

"What's that?"

"I thought about it, and I think I have been neglecting my practice duties as team mom. I want to fill up the water bottles for the team and make sure they are full the entire practice. I'm going to do that every day. Would that be okay?" She began to laugh.

"Sure. Sure. No problem at all."

Shonda started to walk over to the water container but stopped and turned around. "Hey, Coach, how do you like my warm-up suit? Think I will have any complaints today?"

Coach looked the team mom up and down and noticed she was covered from head to toe in a lightweight warm-up suit. "Yeah, you are fine. Just fine."

"Thank you, Coach!"

There was some downtime for Shonda during practice, and it was easy for her to replay the weekend and the "festivities" that she and Coach had partaken in. She was absolutely sure that he got it when she told him that what they were doing was not the norm for her. She believed Coach when he told her that she was the first woman he had been with since the death of his wife and twins. Shonda had no reason not to believe him, especially given how Coach had performed in bed. He was an absolute animal when they got down to it. It was a night of awe for her that she would never forget.

The night they spent together, they reached an amicable agreement that any night they might go out and drink shots, eat wings, or hang out in his truck, it would strictly be their business and they wouldn't place expectations on one another. On more than one occasion Shonda had let Coach know that there had been times in her life when she had spent time with other men and not all of the relationships had ended on good terms. Her revelation didn't seem to faze him one bit. It was therapeutic, because during breaks in the action during their weekend together, she could tell that Coach was having a hard time dealing with the reality that he was with a woman other than his wife.

Shonda didn't press him about it. She couldn't imagine going through his struggle. During their night together, when his mind seemed distant, she would give him his space until he had worked out what was on his mind.

12

Finally, all the hard work at practice came to an end. It was time for the team to show what they were made of in their first game of the season. No one had expected it to happen, but Calvin had fallen so much in love with Theadore Tall's knowledge of football and his stories of the games and players of the sixties that he convinced Coach to sign Mr. Tall on as a coach.

Mr. Tall, the owner of several Laundromat and dry cleaner establishments, had invited so many people from the community to the game that Coach had to commandeer two vans from the motor pool and tell the head of the department it was for a community service day at the park. The day couldn't have been any more perfect, as it was in the seventies, without a hint of the muggy air that had been beating the team down for the past few weeks. At the end of the game the Panthers found themselves on top twenty-eight to fourteen, and as they had done the previous two weeks, Shonda and Coach found a nice little place to celebrate and hang out together.

"You sure do like your shots, don't you?" Coach had just witnessed her take one down.

"I like to chill with some wine sometimes," Shonda revealed. "But tonight isn't that night."

Coach put his shot down and followed it with some brew. "You got that right. We celebrating up in here."

Shonda said, "That's right. The boys played so well."

"I'm not talking about the team right now," he told her.

When his words sank in, she stopped the shot glass at her lips, then put it down. "Well, what are you talking about, then?"

"I'm talking about this. This right here. Me and you, us," he said.

Shonda gave him the look that he enjoyed so much. Wondrous squinted eyes and her sexy smile. "So, you're starting to get some feelings too?"

"Too?" Coach asked.

She said, "Just tell me. Are you starting to dig on ya' team mom?"

They both laughed.

"I am, no doubt," he revealed.

"Well, it hit me too this week at work."

"Really?"

"After one of our phone conversations. I think it was the one when you told me about those football camps J should go to during the summer."

"I remember that."

"I wasn't going to tell you, because we said we were going to keep this one hundred percent friendly, but now look. You're over there spilling your emotions and shit."

"No need to keep pushing it down and it keeps coming back up." Coach picked up his beer.

She picked up her shot glass again to toast.

"To this!" he exclaimed.

"And a lot more of it," Shonda declared.

13

By this time in the season the days were getting darker much earlier, and the scent of fall was all about. After a good practice Calvin, Mr. Tall, and Coach dismissed all the players. They made sure they all had rides home, then began to put the equipment in the storage shed before they went home for the night.

Mr. Tall looked over at Coach as soon as he placed a cooler down in the shed and said, "So, how long you and that team mom been rolling around in the sack?" Mr. Tall didn't have any shame or hesitation.

Instantaneously, Calvin dropped four footballs down in the shed and diverted his attention to Coach. Coach stood still just outside the shed, with the lock in his hand.

"Say what?" Coach asked.

"That's what I'm saying," Calvin added.

Mr. Tall said, "Now, why you want to ask an old man to repeat his words at this stage of his life? You heard me the first time. How long?"

"How long? I didn't even know you were," Calvin said.

"Because it's none of your business," Coach told him.

"Aha! So you *are* spending time with her," Mr. Tall asserted.

Coach could feel Calvin's and Mr. Tall's eyes cutting right through him. "Why are you guys looking at me like that? Calvin, stop looking at me trying to figure out if you should have known all along. And, Mr. Tall, hell no, not today I don't need none of your wisdom, bruh. Just take ya' asses on home."

"Yeah . . . he's been rubbin' feet with her," Mr. Tall observed, deciphering Coach's message.

"Rubbin' feet," Calvin repeated, entertaining himself with Mr. Tall's old-timey reference. "As long as I've known you, Coach, I thought I would have smelled that one out. My brother, you must be really enjoying yourself to not let that cat get out of the bag."

Mr. Tall jumped in. "He knows he has to keep it a secret. Having an affair with a player's mom is dangerous. I'm telling you, dangerous."

Calvin interjected, "That's right. Where is your head at, Coach? You know you're wrong. You better act like you remember my travels down the dark side."

"You took that leap, son?" Mr. Tall wanted to know.

"Actually, I didn't. But a husband said I did. That motherfucka," Calvin scolded. "Had every parent on the team looking at me sideways."

"It's not in a coach's playbook," Mr. Tall said. "Not one play or formation," he added.

Coach finally had to step in. "Look, you two need to relax. All up in my business like it's your own. I got this, man. I will admit, we have been out a few times and like spending time together. Other than that, that's exactly what it is."

"Her son know?" Mr. Tall asked. "By the way he's acting in practice, I say he doesn't."

Mr. Tall's review of the situation made Coach zero in on him. "What do you mean by that?"

"Well, the boy is still working hard, trying to get better. I will bet you dollars to doughnuts that if he knew, he wouldn't be practicing so hard. He would change. Trust me."

Calvin nodded. "He's got a point there."

"Look, you two don't have to worry about it, okay? I got this all under control."

Calvin and Mr. Tall look at each other and decided to drop the subject altogether.

"C'mon, Calvin. Take me home," Mr. Tall said.

Calvin nodded. "Okay. Let's go."

Coach looked at them as they walked away. "Don't be in that car, talking shit about me, with your nosy asses."

Mr. Tall answered, "Fuck you, Coach." And Calvin and Mr. Tall shared a laugh as they began their walk to the car in the falling darkness.

Coach called out, "Uh . . . let's be clear, old man. You ain't known me long enough to talk to me that way."

Over his shoulder Mr. Tall said, "No, *you* be clear. I need to put one of these dusty-ass cleats up your ass for running round with that mama like you doin'."

Calvin told Mr. Tall that he enjoyed hearing the sound of the leaves crunching as he walked to the car and then said, "Can you believe this guy? After he told me to stop drooling over her. Motherfucker."

Mr. Tall put his arm around Calvin. "Oh, by the way, fuck you too, Calvin."

"For what?" Calvin chuckled.

"For saying I look like Redd Foxx in dusty cleats, motherfucka."

Calvin stopped walking and picked up a leaf. "Who told you that?"

Mr. Tall stopped in his tracks, made a fist, pointed his thumb out, and pushed it in the direction of Coach. "Lover boy back there."

They started to walk again.

"I'll be damned. You can't tell a motherfucker shit these days, can you?" Calvin mused, then gave Mr. Tall the leaf and asked him to forgive him as they continued to the car.

14

Coach thought about the words of his coaching staff and realized he had been bit. He had taken the bite hard. He was under an emotional spell, one that he called Shonda. The very minute he walked through the door after practice, he called her and asked Shonda to clear her schedule for the upcoming weekend. It was their bye week; they didn't have a game and he wanted to take her downtown for some fun and time to be alone.

"Damn, Robbie, I don't know if I should be letting you spend your whole check in here, on me, like this." Shonda admitted.

He smiled at Shonda and held up a dress he picked out for her against her body. "Don't worry about how I spend my check, okay?"

She felt his comforting tone. "Okay," she sang.

"And by the way, I like the way you call me Robbie."

"Really?"

"I do."

With another impulsive flirtatious, and sexy moment out the way, Coach watched Shonda as she disappeared into the dressing room with the dress. He couldn't wait until she returned in the all black number that he was sure was going to be perfect for her cocoa complexion. He was happy that he could do this for Shonda and at the same time not have to worry about the money he was spending. He had yet to take a dime of the insurance policy he had on his family. A ten million dollar policy that had been sitting idle in the bank collecting interest for the past three years. It had been easy to continue to live in his old home and pick up his checks at the police station without any distractions that he knew the money would bring if he openly displayed his opulence.

Shonda came out of the dressing room with a smile on her face. Coach had already purchased her five dresses. But this particular dress made her smile unlike all the others. This was the smile he had been searching to see on her face.

"Yes, that's nice baby," he said to her.

"Do you like it?" Shonda took a few steps forward. Then back again. Then she turned around slowly showing all of her curves.

"Of course I do. But the question is . . . do you like?"

"Yes, I like it." She turned to look in the nearby mirror then said, "Baby, since you have known me I have never bragged about myself but I want you to listen to me."

He stepped in closer. "I'm listening."

"Baby, I look good in this dress, I swear I do."

APLW

Team mom / Franklin White.

31182020972435

Wed Feb 10 2021

15

At twenty-eight and raising a son all alone, Shonda Black didn't have too many chances to travel to downtown Atlanta or up to Buckhead to see what they offered. She had never held a grudge about it, because she loved her son. At this point it didn't matter, because she was painting the town now. She promised herself it would not be her first and last time.

"Did you enjoy the room service?" Coach asked.

Shonda moved farther down on the bed, enjoying the thread count. "You know I did," she told him.

He said, "We could have done Ruth's Chris. . . . As a matter of fact, if you want to go over there for a drink, we can."

"Uh-uh. I'm good right here in this bed, next to you, sipping on this wine and looking at the view of the city."

Coach asked Shonda if she was sure she was okay.

"Yes. Who would have thought yesterday that tonight I would be on club level at the InterContinental Hotel? You have outdone yourself, sir."

They were both looking out at the skyline. They had to be looking south, because they could see downtown Atlanta clearly.

"I owe Jarques's friend's mother, Jackie, such a huge favor for letting Jarques stay over."

"Yes, she helped to make this happen," Coach replied.

Shonda sat up a bit. "Wow. I just thought of something. Pretty soon he will be able to just stay at home alone if

Mama wants to get away," she mused. "Hell, college is knocking on the door, if you want to get technical." She had some of her wine. "I hope he's ready for all that."

Coach was looking directly at his beauty queen. "We talk to them about that all the time. It's just not football with us. We are trying to get these young men to under-stand that going to college is the best choice in these times, and that's if you're playing football or not."

Shonda told Coach, "And that's exactly why I brought him over to your team, because that is the word on the streets about you. The word is that you care."

"People say that about me?"

"You're a legend, baby." She began to laugh; then she returned to the topic at hand. "It's just that since he was a little boy, I have tried to tell him that whatever he wants in life, he can get it if he works at it, but I have always wondered if those words would mean more coming from a man."

"I grew up with my mom," Coach revealed.

Shonda could see Coach go back into his memory bank. She would never forget how he looked after telling her about his wife and kids. That night, even through the darkness, his pain was so clear.

Coach was looking back at the skyline now. "But my pops, he was always around, but not *around*. You know what I mean? Come in some days or . . . not. He wasn't too talkative. Not one word about girls or what it meant to be a man. I think he thought that my seeing him every once in a while was good enough, because, you know, none of my friends had their dads, either."

"So, you never heard those words coming out of a man's mouth, either?"

"No."

"And you've done very well with your life. So it's possible," Shonda said, realization dawning.

"Sure it is."

Coach and Shonda sat looking at the city in silence.

A few minutes later Coach said out of the blue, "Maybe we should tell J about us."

She turned to him, her wineglass still in her hand.

Coach made himself clear. "I would like to tell your son about us. Then I can help you get the message to him about achievement and goals. You know, lead by example on a daily basis."

Shonda looked deep into his eyes for what seemed like minutes. Coach was not sure if he had made her upset, especially when her eyes began to tear.

"You okay?"

Shonda cleared her throat before she spoke. "Coach, listen, I have made a lot of mistakes in my life. I mean, a lot. Look at me. Had a child at fourteen, didn't make his father accept responsibility, and was crazy enough to think I could do it all by myself. Do you know I have practically cried myself to sleep every night for the last fourteen years? So . . . when you ask me something like that, I feel good, but I get very protective."

The look on Coach's face told Shonda he didn't understand.

"Look, when Jarques finally realized that he wasn't going to have a dad in his life, I went out and tried to find a man who could fill the void—another one of my mistakes in life. I mean, I have never had a problem with men approaching me and wanting to get to know me, and there were times when I would go with a man and after the first few dates try to push my son on him, and it made men resent me. It made men resent him too and exhibit all types of hatred because he was in the way. They knew the only way to me was to put up with him, in the right way, not just any way. So, when you tell me you want to teach him things, I get protective because I don't want it to be because you want to get next to me. You already have me."

Coach said, "I understand. I understand everything you're saying. Just know that I was going to be a father. And I couldn't wait to be a father. I get what you're saying. I want to do it because it needs to be done. And that's the only reason why."

16

Shonda's plan the next day was to pick up her son, Jarques, from his friend's house and then go home. However, she was in such a good mood that after Jarques got in the car, she got on I-20 west and headed to Six Flags for a day of fun with him. They hadn't been there since he was eight or nine years old, and once she thought about it, she realized this could be the last time they would ever go together. Time was just beginning to move by so quickly, and like she told Coach, soon he would be on his way to college.

Shonda enjoyed the park much more when Jarques was a little boy and the only rides he could go on were ones she could stomach. While they were at the park, her son had her on so many different stomach-churning, floor-dropping, fast-moving machines that she thought she would lose her mind. When they finally were home, she retreated to her bedroom and lay down, trying to rest and get her faculties back in order because she had to go to work in the morning. She knew the doorbell would be ringing soon, but she was so out of it that when it did, Jarques had to answer the door.

"Hey, Coach," Jarques said.

"What's up, J? You doing all right?"

The young buck nodded his head. "You here to see my mom about something for the team? 'Cause she's asleep right now."

"Actually, I came to see you."

Jarques looked at Coach. "Me?"

"Yeah. C'mon out on the porch so we can chat."

Jarques had his Madden game on full blast and looked back at the television screen, then back at Coach. Reluctantly, he went out on the porch to see what Coach wanted.

The porch was actually only big enough for one person to stand on, so Coach stood right before the first step and Jarques stood on the top step. The boy gazed down his street to check out what was going on before he looked directly at Coach.

"So . . . how is everything today?" Coach wanted to know.

Jarques wondered what Coach wanted. He was waiting for Coach to continue, but whatever Coach had to say didn't come out fast enough, so Jarques asked him right out the reason behind his visit. "Coach, did you come over here to tell me that you were going out with my mom?"

Jarques's question seemed to make Coach swallow whatever words he was trying to get out of his mouth. He cleared his throat. "How'd you know that? I mean, yes, yes, that's why I'm here," he said.

"Okay," Jarques told him.

"Okay?" Coach repeated.

"Yeah, okay. I was wondering if you were going to say something or just keep acting like it wasn't happening."

Coach said, "No, no. I mean, I wanted to come to you like a man."

"Okay."

"So, you're okay with it?" Coach wanted to know.

"Yeah, I said, 'Okay.'"

There was a very awkward moment of silence.

Jarques gazed down the street again. "Uh, Coach, I don't really want to be seen out here just staring at you."

Coach looked around. "Okay, yeah. Right."

"See you at practice," Jarques told him, right before he turned around to go back in the house.

Coach reached for him but didn't make contact. "J, wait a minute. Tell me something. How'd you know? How'd you know we were going out?"

Jarques took a deep breath. "Really, Coach?"

"Yeah, really. Tell me."

Jarques looked up and down the street again, then exhaled. "Okay, I'll put it like this. I knew something was up when she started making me breakfast every morning."

Coach was listening intently. "Oh, okay . . . breakfast. Got it."

"Yeah, that's right. And I knew because when I came home from practice, dinner was always made. I knew because she started to whisper on the phone and bring home leftovers from weird places. I knew because she's been listening to music and singing along as it plays. I knew because she's been trying to help me with my homework, and I don't even need it. I knew because if I made a very small mistake, like forgetting to put my plate up or taking out the trash, she wouldn't yell at me about it. I knew because every day is a day of encouragement, so much so that I can barely stand it. And I knew because every day she's been waking up with a smile on her face and she seems happy. That's how I knew, Coach. And guess what, Coach?"

Coach was blown away. "Yeah, yeah? What's that?"

"I've seen this all before . . . so, Coach?"

"I'm listening."

"Don't fuck this up, 'cause living with her now, it's how it's supposed to be."

17

For a few days Coach was able to get back into his normal routine of work, community meetings, and football practice afterward. The team had a big game coming up that could determine their position in the play-offs, so making sure the team understood that was on his mind. Earlier in the day, he'd sent flowers over to Shonda at her job. He'd signed the card, "Your secret admirer," so when his cell phone started to ring while he sat at his desk, he was pretty sure he was seconds away from hearing her voice and answered the call.

A voice said back to him, "Damn, boy, you sure are answering that phone in a sexy way."

Coach took the phone off his ear and looked at it, then placed it back so he could speak. "What? Who is this?"

"Put it like this, sexy man. I'm not who you wanted it to be." There was a laugh afterward.

Coach realized who it was. "Mr. Tall, what do you want?"

"Hey, hope you're not busy, because I need you to come out to the neighborhood. A friend of mine, her house was broken into last night, when she was sleeping. When she woke up, they told her to stay in the bed and go back to sleep, or they'd whoop her like they used to do back in slavery."

"They broke in while she was sleeping?"

Mr. Tall said, "She lives down the street from me. I'll meet you at my house as soon as you can, because I already told her you were on the way."

Coach rushed to remind Mr. Tall that he did not patrol the streets anymore. "Look, I'm a public relations officer. I'm not on the street anymore. . . ." There was silence on the other end. He removed the phone from his ear, looked at it, put it back to his ear, and then said, "Hello? Hello?"

It took Coach about five minutes to rearrange the time of a planned meeting and leave the station to meet with Mr. Tall. When he pulled up in his police cruiser, Mr. Tall was standing in the driveway in a peacoat and small brown tweed apple hat, with his hands in his pockets, fighting off the chill of the day. Coach parked the car at the curb in front of the house and stepped out, leaving the door open and the car running.

Coach called, "C'mon. Get in. I'll drive you down."

"Uh-uh," Mr. Tall answered.

Coach was a bit agitated. The pitch of his voice was much higher than normal. "Mr. Tall, say what?"

Mr. Tall said, "Let's walk."

"Walk?" Coach repeated, then looked at his watch and then back at Mr. Tall.

"Yeah. So whoever is doing this might see you."

Coach looked at his police car, then back at Mr. Tall again. "Are they blind or some shit? 'Cause I'm in a black and white."

"C'mon, man . . . let's walk. I'm telling you, I know this neighborhood."

Coach got back in his car with an attitude now, turned it off, grabbed his jacket, hopped out, and shut the door. "Which way?"

"Down this way." Mr. Tall gestured with his hand, then looked over at Coach. "Look, listen here. Where's your gun?"

Coach followed Mr. Tall's eyes and looked down at his waist, then back at Mr. Tall. "My gun?"

"Yeah. Where is it?"

"I need a gun? If I need a gun, I got to call for some backup, man."

Mr. Tall said, "Probably not. I just want to know where yours is."

"I don't carry it," Coach said, looking down the street.

"And you're on the police force?"

"Yup," Coach answered.

"With no gun?"

"That's what I said."

"You ever heard of sitting ducks?" Mr. Tall asked.

"Of course I have."

"Well, we're what you call sitting bitches. C'mon. Let's get our asses down this street before we get fucked up," Mr. Tall said.

18

During their walk down the street, which was called Blue Ridge Lane, Mr. Tall gave Coach the name of every person who lived on the block, along with a breakdown of those who at one time had lived in a few of the vacant homes up and down the street. It took only a few minutes to get to their destination. They walked up the driveway of the all-brick home with the nice, well-kept yard.

Mr. Tall paused before he knocked on the door.

"Be cool, man. At one time or another me and her . . . well, you know."

When the door opened, a small woman who had long black hair and who looked to be of Indian decent appeared. She smiled. "Theadore, as always you kept your word. Is this your friend?" she asked right before she let them in.

Coach introduced himself. Told her he was with the police department. She told him her name was Lois Gregory and she was a retired schoolteacher. Then she led them into her living room and invited them to sit. Coach took a quick look around and noticed lots of photos in frames.

She wanted to be clear about Coach's identity. "So this is the officer, Theadore?"

"Yes, indeed. This is him. He is police. I work with him down on the field."

She surveyed Coach. "So where's your gun?"

Coach inched up on the couch to make himself more comfortable. "Ma'am, I work in public relations for the police department." Then he looked at Mr. Tall and frowned. "As a matter of fact, I have been working with this community, this neighborhood, to try to put a stop to all the break-ins. We've had a few meetings. Have you attended?"

Lois shook her head. "I wish I could have attended. But I can't. It seems every time I leave this place, my house is either broken into or some type of damage happens to it. I don't know who is doing it, but they are just like those terrorists that they are talking about on the news."

"Do you have any idea who might be doing this?" Coach asked.

"Nope." She looked at Mr. Tall, then back at Coach. "You're the police, right?"

Coach nodded. "Yes. I promote the department and hear community concerns."

"Oh, really?" she said.

"Yes, ma'am."

"Well, if you ask me, if the community concerns were taken care of, that would be a hell of a promotion for the police department, no?"

Coach said, "I understand, but I just take the information I have to submit it to those who work the streets."

Lois became quiet, drawing everyone in the room in. Then she said, "Things just can't be like this. They can't. Do you have a mother, Officer?"

"She passed some years ago," Coach told her.

"Well, God bless her soul," she said. "But tell me, how would you feel if she was afraid to leave her home or to go to sleep at night? You know, I thought about getting a dog. But a dog can't live inside here forever. He has to get out too. This is where I live, and I need to feel safe. Now these hoodlums break into my home, walk around in it while I'm sleeping, and tell me to be quiet, or they are going to beat me like they used to do back in slavery. This has to stop. Now."

Coach sat with Lois and Mr. Tall for over an hour. She told Coach how in her younger days she had envisioned living when she became a senior citizen and how she was actually living now were worlds apart. Coach didn't like the fact that a woman who'd given so many years of her life to teaching kids was being taken advantage of by those she had most likely taught at one time or another. But because his job was in public relations, all he could do was listen and let her know that he would try his best to make sure that those who worked the streets made her neighborhood safe again.

19

When Coach returned to the department, he walked right into the watch commander's office without knocking and sat down.

The watch commander didn't even budge as he typed on an old typewriter. When he finished, he looked over at Coach and stared with more than evil eyes before he spoke.

He said, "You forgot to put those vans back on full, motherfucker."

Coach shook his head. "Yeah, yeah, I'll get to it."

"So what you want? Can't you see I'm busy? I can't tell you how much this place is getting on my freakin' nerves."

"Need to talk," Coach told him.

"'Bout what?"

"Crime."

The watch commander said, "Crime? Ain't this a bitch. I thought you were coming in here to discuss world politics and shit. What do you want, Rob? I have things to do."

"Look, I've been holding meetings in the neighborhood. We need to double up the patrols day and night. These fucking thugs are terrorizing people so bad, they don't want to come out of their homes."

The watch commander took off his glasses and rubbed his eyes. His voice was strained from the pressure of the day when he spoke. "You think we don't know that?"

Coach said, "I know you know, because I keep telling you."

"And I keep telling you, we can use only what we have. We have only so many police to patrol the streets, and until somebody in that big-ass office over there comes in here and tells us we have another hundred cops to put a stop to this shit, then guess what? The fucking shit continues."

They sat and stared at one another in silence.

Finally, Coach said, "You ever thought about getting off your ass and walking over there, letting them know what's really going on in these streets, Brent?"

"Look, I've tried. I have done my job. Everybody's shit is packed right now. If I go over there with some more shit, then guess what I become? That's right. Their problem. And when they get problems in that big office over there, they get rid of them as soon as they can so they don't have to hear it. Look at me here, I'm typing on a fuckin' typewriter in this day and age because they don't want to fix my computer."

There was another stare down between the two, and then the watch commander continued with his paper-work.

Coach found some energy to put up a fight. "This is bullshit. Senior citizens shouldn't have to live like this."

The watch commander looked up. "Save it." He put his glasses back on and then placed another sheet of paper in the typewriter without another word. When Coach got up to leave, the watch commander stopped him.

"Yeah?" Coach said.

"Maybe it's time for you to come off of the sidelines and get back in the game."

Coach said, "What are you talking about?"

"You know exactly what I'm talking about. My sister told me firsthand that you two had insurance policies on one another."

"So what does that mean?"

"It means that you have become complacent. Walking around on cruise control now. It's been a while now since that drunken bastard killed baby girl and the twins. I see you every day, and you come in here because you're still trying to keep busy, and it's not doing anybody any good, 'cause you're not making a difference. Hell, you have enough money that you could walk the world if you wanted. So, if you don't want to do something that matters, your ass should just go . . . and see what else the world has to offer."

Coach said, "What's wrong with coming in here and staying busy?"

"Nothing wrong with it. It's not you, though."

"Come again?"

"That's not the man my sister married. If that was your MO, I wouldn't have let her marry your sorry ass."

Coach said, "Is that right?"

"Gotdamn right. Move on, man. You can get back on these streets anytime you want. I only put you in this got-damned position until you got your head right, anyway."

Coach and his dead wife's brother looked each other straight in the eye. Coach said, "I hear you. I hear you." Then he walked out.

As Coach moved down the hallway, his brother-in-law, the watch commander, screamed, "Okay, if you hear me, don't forget to fill up my gotdamned vans!"

20

After Shonda called Coach and talked him up nonstop about how much she liked the flowers, Coach sat down at his desk and tried to come up with a plan to help Ms. Lois Gregory and stop all the break-ins happening in the neighborhood.

In addition to that, he began to deal with himself. For the past year, every time he told someone that he would make sure something was done or he would look into it, he'd gotten a bad feeling inside. The sentiment came from knowing deep down that if he had to go to someone within the police department to get it done, the shit was not getting completed. It had gotten to the point that when he would take the concerns of citizens to various individuals, it felt like he was talking and they were looking back at him like he was a damn fool.

Coach thought that maybe the watch commander was right. Why not get back on the streets and try to make things better if he could? Still, he was sure that the commander's words were laced with encouragement. He was right about one thing: his sister didn't marry a punk, and every time something became difficult when she was in his life, he faced it straight up and did what needed to be done. Coach didn't have to think too long about his decision before he marched back into the watch commander's office and told him that tonight he was putting his street uniform back on and he would do so until they found out who the hell was dealing out havoc in the community.

***

"Wow. It's been way too long since I had a dinner like this," Coach said. He was sitting at the dinner table with Shonda and Jarques.

"I'm glad you like it." Shonda was all smiles. She felt good about the meal she had prepared. She cut a piece of the baked chicken and plopped it in her mouth.

Jarques cut in. "My grandmother . . . she taught my mama how to cook."

"You remember that, Jarques?" Shonda asked, a smile still on her face.

"Yup. I remember you didn't want to, but she wouldn't cook unless you helped."

Coach had some ice water, then placed the glass back down. "Okay, getting back to our conversation, J, there is no way that the song 'All I Want For My Birthday Is a Big Booty Girl' is a classic."

Shonda laughed, then agreed.

Jarques said, "Yes, it is. . . . They used to play it on the radio almost every ten or twenty minutes and for your information the name of the song is 'Birthday Song'."

"Oh, so because they play it on the radio every two seconds, that makes it a classic?" Coach asked.

Jarques nodded. "Yup."

"Why is that?"

"Because if they didn't, so many people wouldn't know about it."

Coach thought for a moment, then said, "Yeah, okay. I get it."

Coach didn't bother to question Jarques too much more about his taste in music after that. He just enjoyed the atmosphere at the dinner. It was clear that Shonda was happy that her son knew she was trying to get on with her life and still care for him too. And Coach was happy because for so many nights in the past three years, he had eaten dinner alone, with thoughts of what could have been dancing in his head.

After dinner, Coach wanted to drive past Ms. Lois Gregory's home to make sure she was okay. Since things were going well that evening, he went out on a limb and asked Jarques if he wanted to ride with him. This would give Jarques firsthand experience riding in a police car, in the front seat, for that matter. Jarques didn't seem that interested but agreed to go after his mother gave him a little nudging and after Coach promised they would return in twenty minutes, tops.

21

Jarques said, "So, criminals sit back there?"

It had been a minute since Coach had been in a reg-istered cruiser with all the bells and whistles, and he fumbled with the squelch on the radio, because it was too loud. "Yeah, all kinds of badasses," he replied. This car was much different from the Taurus he'd been driving.

Jarques watched him continue to fumble with the radio. "You sure you know what you're doing, Coach?"

Coach looked at him. "Yeah, I do."

Jarques said, "Doesn't look like it."

The cruiser's siren blared suddenly, and Jarques's mother opened the door to the house and looked out. "Is everything okay out here?"

Coach had to answer Shonda by rolling down the window and shouting over Jarques's laughter that they were fine. Finally, everything was exactly the way Coach wanted it. "There . . . I got it. It's been a minute, you know?"

Jarques said, "Yeah, I can tell."

Coach could tell Jarques was excited, but not in curious way. "You okay?"

"Yeah," Jarques said. Then he changed his mind. "No, not really."

"What's on your mind?" Coach said.

"Just wondering why somebody would want a job that locks people up in jail." He was still looking around the car.

Coach hesitated before answering. "You know, that's a good question."

"Yeah?"

"That's part of the reason I took a desk job," Coach confessed.

"What's the other part?"

Coach negotiated a left-hand turn and looked over at Jarques. "I lost my family," he said. "Lost them in a car accident. I wasn't coping too well in the streets."

Jarques didn't react. He didn't know what to say. Coach could even feel him tighten up.

"It's okay, J. It's been a few years now, and I'm coming back around."

There was a brief pause in their conversation. Coach was listening to some of the calls on the radio. Jarques was halfway listening to the radio and looking out the window of the car.

"So, where are we going again?"

"To check on a neighborhood where some citizens have been robbed repeatedly."

Jarques looked to the left and to the right as they drove down the street and straightened up, paying attention, then looked over at Coach. "You have your guns, right?"

"Guns?"

Jarques sort of chuckled. "Yes, guns. Every time I see cops, they have guns. Rifles and all that." He looked around again. "Where's yours, Coach?"

"Didn't get them yet. Not until morning, when I get a reissue."

"So we're riding over there without guns?" Jarques asked, trying to understand.

"Yup."

Jarques remained quiet, and Coach could feel the boy's eyes on him as he drove.

It didn't take Coach more than seven minutes to arrive at the neighborhood where all the robberies were taking place. He was around the corner from Mr. Tall's and Lois Gregory's places. He slowed the car down after he turned onto their street.

"This must be it, right?" Jarques questioned.

"Yeah," Coach replied.

"I could tell. You slowed down, and I heard the gravel under the tires, just like in the movies."

"Is that right?" Coach was impressed.

"Yeah."

"You're very observant. Maybe you have a future in police work."

"Nah, doubt it," Jarques quickly replied.

Coach was moving slowly down the street. He took a spotlight from the middle of the seat and shone it on each house they passed, making sure everything was safe.

"Coach, so if you don't have a gun, what're you going to do if you see someone?"

"Call it in on the radio, son," Coach replied.

It was quiet for a moment. Then Jarques said, "You know, I've never been called that before by a man."

Coach was looking out at the homes, still shining the spotlight on them. "Called what?"

It was quiet again for another moment. "Son," Jarques told him.

Coach put down the spotlight and put his foot on the brake. "I'm sorry. . . . I mean, it just came out."

Jarques smiled. "It's cool. Just wanted you to know."

Coach said, "You sure?"

"Yeah, I'm sure," Jarques said, and then he looked back out the window.

Coach looked at him. Another second and he would have been staring. "Oh, okay . . . good."

It was dark, but most of the homes they passed still had lights on inside, as most people were more than likely finishing up with dinner and getting ready for the next day. As Coach swung his spotlight back and forth across the street, shining it on each house, someone ran across the street, and he stopped the car.

Jarques turned and looked at Coach.

"You see that?" Coach asked.

"Yeah."

"Someone just ran across the street." Coach moved the spotlight in the direction in which they saw the person run, and when the spotlight caught up with him, they saw a group of boys standing on the sidewalk. Coach sat still for a moment, then started driving forward. When the boys saw the car moving toward them, they started walking so that their backs were facing the car.

Coach didn't pick up speed. He just kept driving along, and the spotlight lit them all up when he caught up to them. Each and every one of the boys turned their heads away from the car and looked as though they were seconds away from taking off running. Coach didn't stop. He just rolled by, keeping the spotlight on them, and as they approached the corner of the street, all the boys made a right and continued on their way.

"You think those were the guys?" Jarques said.

"I don't know. Could be."

"Didn't look like they were doing nothing to me but walking," Jarques said.

"Yeah." Coach sat at the corner until the boys were no longer in sight, then made a left. Directly across the street on the main strip, Jarques noticed a small mom-and-pop shop.

"Oh, cool. Can you pull in there so I can get some candy for tomorrow?"

He asked the question so quickly that Coach didn't have time to think about it. When he pulled into the lot, he put the car in park. "Sure your mama lets you take candy to school?"

"Yeah, she lets me all the time. It keeps me focused."

Coach looked up at the store. "Focused, right. Boy, don't get me in any trouble. Okay, hurry up. I told your mother we would be back in twenty minutes."

Jarques ran into the store, and Coach dialed up Mr. Tall. He answered on the second ring.

"Hey. It's Coach."

Mr. Tall said, "Hey. What did you do? Decide to let me change that counter play?"

"No, that's not happening. I wanted you to know that I'm in a police cruiser and just drove past your street and everything looks good out your way."

"You're in a cruiser?"

"Yeah."

Mr. Tall wanted to know what was going on. "With another officer? Somebody with a gun?"

"No, my assigned car. I'm getting back on the street, Tall."

"What? What did I miss?" Mr. Tall asked, because the last he'd heard, Coach didn't want anything to do with the streets.

"Just felt like it's the right thing to do, at least until we find out what's going on."

Mr. Tall said, "Well, that's good to know, because Ms. Lois and I have been wondering all day what we are going to do, and more than likely, she's going to move in here with me for a while."

"Oh, really?" Coach inquired.

"Yes, sir. Says she will not wake up again with a bunch of fools running all through her home, threatening her and all. It will be good for her."

Coach noticed Jarques come out of the store. "Okay, I will talk to you later about it. Got to go." Coach waited for Jarques to get in the car.

Right before Jarques opened the car door, he looked up and caught sight of the group of boys that Coach had shined the spotlight on. He didn't speak to them or nod or do anything like that. He just looked on as one of the boys in the crew nodded at him, acknowledging him.

Coach looked back and noticed the crew as Jarques got in the car.

"You okay?"

"Yeah," Jarques responded.

"You know them?" Coach said.

"Nah . . ."

22

When they walked in the door, Jarques went to his room, and Shonda and Coach enjoyed some time in the back room, on the couch, remaining there almost until David Letterman was done with his routine.

"You know I want you to stay, don't you?" Shonda said. She was beginning to cuddle up real nice like.

Coach felt her hand move down to his lap. "Yeah, I can tell."

"So why don't you?"

She put her soft brown lips back on his for the second or third time.

"As much as I want to, I can't."

"Oh, yes, you can." Shonda put her leg over his.

He laughed. "Uh-uh. No, I can't."

"Robbie . . ."

"Don't want to disrespect J like that. Believe it or not, he'll be a man soon enough, and what I show him now, he's going to be taking notes on."

The couple began to kiss again until they could barely continue without ripping off each other's clothes.

"I better go," Coach said.

"Yes, you better, before I take you right here," Shonda told him.

Coach's plan was to get home and get ready for a big day, the next day on the job. He knew he had to be reissued his street gear, and there would probably be more than enough ribbing from the guys on the force than he could stand. He realized he would have to change his entire demeanor now that he had been on the inside and was going back out. He knew what being on the outside did to him. It made him angry, impatient, and full of sadness at the same time. This was a chance to prove to himself that he didn't have to become angry at the system and to overcome the loss of his family without taking it out on someone else.

After Shonda sent him home after one last kiss, Coach got into the car. The feeling he experienced at that moment was close to the excitement teenagers routinely felt. He felt charged and rejuvenated by Shonda's encouragement to get back on the streets and do what he'd been doing for the thirteen years before his family's accident set him back. Getting back on the streets wasn't going to be hard to do, because while at work Coach had kept his eyes and ears peeled on all the other officers and knew what they were going through. Plus, he had continued to go to the shift meetings, so he was always in the loop.

In order to get home, Coach had to go in Mr. Tall's direction again. Another drive-by seemed like a good idea, as he was still getting used to the patrol car. When he drove past Mr. Tall's home, the light was on in one of the front rooms, and he smiled because he knew that Mr. Tall was probably inside talking shit to Ms. Lois about how good a football player he used to be. After passing Mr. Tall's house, he drove down to Ms. Lois's home, backed into her driveway, and sat there for thirty minutes, just listening to the chatter on the police radio and keeping a watch. Thankfully, his watch was without incident.

23

The next morning, hours before the shift meeting, Coach was back at the department and ready for duty. He walked to the watch commander's office, tapped on the door, and walked in. The watch commander was barely awake and looked up at the sight before his eyes. Before Coach could say one word, the watch commander broke into a boisterous laugh, and Coach stood there, wondering what it was all about.

"How long did it take you to polish those shoes?" the watch commander asked.

"What're you talking about?" Coach said.

"And that gotdamned dress uniform. Where the fuck are you going?"

"Hey, it's my first day back on the job. I'm just respecting my position," Coach informed him.

"Your position?"

"Damn right. My position."

The watch commander stood up from his desk and walked over to Coach and checked him out some more. "You sure look good."

Coach looked down at his shoes then tugged on his jacket, smoothing out his uniform. He was really proud of himself now. "Thanks."

"But you better take this shit off," the watch commander told him and began to laugh again.

Coach said, "What the hell are you talking about? I'm back on the streets today."

"Go and take this shit off and get into a suit. You're a detective now."

"A detective?"

The watch commander walked back behind his desk and stood there with a smile on his face. "That's right." He pulled a detective's badge out of one of his desk drawers. "This fucking thing has been in here since . . . well, you know. You made detective the same day. I just pushed it aside. Congrats, Detective." The watch commander held out his hand to give Coach the badge.

Coach didn't move.

"Here. Take it. You deserve it. By the way, you'll be one of the first to get one of those new Chevy Caprices. They'll be here in the morning. The damn thing has three hundred fifty-five horses inside, you lucky bastard. At least headquarters has gotten something right."

A gotdamned detective. Coach hated surprises, and his brother in-law knew that, but he really enjoyed this one. Back in the day, before the tragedy, becoming a detective was one of his main goals. While he'd told his wife that his life as a street cop wouldn't be forever, it had taken until this moment for all his efforts on the streets to pay off. And to know that this slot had been there for him ever since the tragedy . . . Coach had to try to wrap his mind around being a detective. He hadn't thought about it one time since he lost his wife. It was hard for him to even remember thinking about how he would tackle the position. When he was a regular police officer who drove a squad car with one of his twenty partners in thirteen years on duty, he would visualize himself walking into crime scenes and solving cases. Coach was pleasantly surprised to find out that his work before the accident was being recognized.

The watch commander told him that he was expected to get his feet wet nice and slow. He was to finish up any pressing business he had in public relations, and then he would be assigned the task of tracking down those responsible for the home break-ins and the terrorist-style threat that was handed out to Ms. Lois Gregory. Coach didn't know it, but Lois had informed the county commissioners about the threat too. It turned out that Lois knew many of the younger commissioners who lived in the area as they had had her for a teacher. Those high-level suits weren't pleased, and they wanted answers and an arrest made as soon as possible to show their respect for her.

24

One thing Coach did remember about wanting to be a detective was the fact that every time he stepped into the street to investigate a crime, he wanted to be sharp and dressed to the nines. The upgrade to detective was a code word for suit shopping and lots of it. With a game coming up on Saturday, Sunday would be his first chance to get a suit, or two or three, or probably four. Coach was going to need more time. So he decided that he would take the next day off and go shopping. Given the educational value of watching a man go through the process of being fitted for a suit, he thought it would be a good thing for Jarques to tag along with him. And he'd make sure that Jarques got fitted too. But first, Coach had to convince Shonda to let Jarques accompany him.

"Take him out of school?" This was about as loud as Coach had heard Shonda's voice.

"Yeah. It's an educational trip," he replied.

"To do what again?"

"Show the boy how a man shops. Show him how to get fitted for a suit and buy shoes, shirts, and ties."

"What do you mean? You just go to the store and pick one off the rack and go to church." That had been the norm for Shonda. It was a quick and worry-free way of shopping.

"See, that's what I'm talking about," Coach said. "That is not how you properly purchase a suit. He needs to get fitted. Let the seamstress or tailor measure his chest, arms, and legs so the suit will fit him just right. Then he has to see what type of cut looks good on him, what he likes. It takes longer than fifteen minutes to get a suit. Trust me, he will never forget it, and he needs to know how to do this."

Shonda still had questions. "Are you serious?"

"Yes, and let's not forget about the shoes, shirts, and ties. This is going to be an all-day affair. We are going to have to be out and about as soon as the stores open if we are going to get everything we need."

"All this because you made detective?" Shonda asked.

"Yes. Plus, we'll have a chance to hang out."

"Okay, but I don't want you to buy him a lot of stuff."

"What's a lot?"

"Bags full of stuff, so much that he begins to think he's a man himself."

Coach laughed. "I keep telling you he practically is, but I'll make sure he gets a couple of suits and some shoes, okay?"

"That's it?"

"That's it."

25

Lois had been looking in Mr. Tall's backyard that morning. When she saw the grill that he'd told her he had made by hand, it reminded her of the ribs and barbecue chicken he would bring down to her house from time to time. Since it was the end of the week. Lois talked Mr. Tall into barbecuing some ribs on the oversize grill in his backyard.

Mr. Tall enjoyed Lois's cooking as well. She always had healthy helpings of black-eyed peas and collard greens at the ready. Lois let him know that she had both in her freezer down at her house and that it would be a good time to go get them as they could thaw them and put everything together for a tasty meal.

Things had never been so weird for Lois. She had lived in her house for over thirty years, and now she was sneaking in and out because she didn't feel safe living there all alone. She wanted to get a little me time and enjoy the beautiful weather, so she told Mr. Tall she'd be back later as he started to wipe down the grill and place some charcoal inside it.

As she walked down the street, she encountered two neighbors who were outside. One was sitting in a lawn chair close to his garage, and the other was walking around in circles in the yard with his dog. She stopped to engage in small talk with them. They both knew what was going on in the neighborhood and let her know that they'd been keeping an eye out. Her neighbor with the dog even let her know that he had noticed a police car in her driveway the other night, which made Lois feel a little better.

When Lois stepped inside her home, the first thing she remembered was that she wanted to turn off the air-conditioning. The nights were becoming a lot cooler, and she had decided to run the ceiling fans in place of the air-conditioning, which would keep the house fresh during the day while saving money on the electric bill. She made her way over to one of the ceiling fans and turned it on. The control to the air conditioner was right beside it, and she turned it off.

"I like the air-conditioning better. These ceiling fans fuck with my sinuses," a male voice said.

Lois gasped and placed her hand on her chest, as she could see someone with his back toward her. He was sitting in the high-back chair in her living room. The same chair in which she watched her favorite TV shows and read her novels. Her first instinct was to get out of the house as fast as possible, but the moment she turned to leave, she was stopped by a person standing between her and the door.

"You going somewhere?"

Lois looked up at the person holding her by the arm. She couldn't see his face, because he was wearing a white mask and a baseball cap. He forced her to turn around.

"Get your hand off me!" she said as forcefully as she could.

"Or what? Yo, do you hear this bitch telling me what to do?" the masked punk said.

Lois could tell by his voice that he was young.

There was laughter coming from the living room, from the person still sitting in her chair.

She could tell that he was a young male too, and although she couldn't see their faces, she realized from their voices that they were the ones who had threatened her before.

"What? What is it you want, and why are you in my house again?"

"*Your* house?" the masked one asked.

"Yes, *my* house, and I said, 'Get your hands off me.'" She tried to pull away.

"This is *my* house, bitch," he said. "And we needed someplace to stay the night. We thought you'd be down the street again with your boyfriend. Next time you decide to come down here, you ought to let us know." When he cursed her, she wasn't surprised.

"You know, your mother should have taught you better than this," Lois told him.

"Well, she didn't. Now what?"

"You should go back and tell her that she wronged you, boy. That's what."

He looked over her head and into the living room, at the one in the chair. "Yo, you hear this bitch?"

"Your mother was pretty trifling, though."

They both laughed some.

"See? Everyone knows," Lois said.

Lois looked at the door, and the masked one caught her in the act and turned to the door and turned the knob to the dead bolt. "Don't even think about it," he said.

"Yo, bring her in here and keep a lookout," the home invader sitting in the living room yelled out to his partner.

The masked one grabbed Lois by the arm, dragged her in front of his partner sitting in her chair, then took up position behind her drapes, covering the window, to keep an eye out.

"That's my favorite chair," Lois said.

The punk in the chair laughed a little.

"I don't know why you are sitting in it with a mask over your face. I already know who you are," she told him.

"So you know who I am?"

"Yes, I do."

"You seem to know a lot, don't you?"

Lois didn't back down. "I know who you are. I know that much."

"What else do you know?"

Lois didn't understand the question and didn't answer back.

He made it clear to her. "Do you know why that police car sat in your driveway last night?"

"Probably looking for you," she said without hesitation.

"If they wanted me, they could have come inside and got me. How do they know about me, anyway?"

"I told them, that's how. If you're old enough to make threats, then you're old enough to handle what comes after that."

This guy didn't respond, and that forced the punk looking out the window to glance back at him.

Lois looked at both of them before she spoke. "I don't know what's wrong with you boys today," she said. "Do you really think you can just threaten people and come in their home because you feel like it and take it over?"

The punk at the window turned around. "Looks like I can, don't it?"

"But you're going to get caught, and when you do, I'm going to be there to watch you get put in jail," Lois promised.

"You sure of that?"

"There is no doubt about it," Lois said. By now she was fed up with being a hostage in her own home, and she ran for the door.

The young intruder who was sitting sprang out of the chair and grabbed her by the arm. "Where do you think you're going?"

"Get out of here!" Lois yelled at him. "Get out!"

"We will get out when you finally answer the question that man asked you," said the punk at the window.

"Question? What question?" She struggled to free herself.

"Whose house is this?" said the punk who had grabbed her. He was now squeezing her arm harder and harder by the second. Then, without warning, he punched her in the face. "I said, whose house is this?" And he punched her again and again and again.

26

It took some heavy persuasion to convince Jarques that a day out with Coach to learn the art of shopping for a suit, along with all its accessories, was a step toward manhood that he needed to take sooner than later. Jarques used every excuse imaginable not to go. He even let Shonda and Coach know that he had a test during first period at school that he just couldn't miss. Shonda decided to let him go to school for the test and arranged for Coach to pick him up afterward for his day of enlightening.

On their day of shopping, Coach and Jarques walked out of the school together. Coach nodded at his new ride while at the same time putting his driver's license back in his pocket. He'd used it as identification to sign Jarques out of school.

"Wow. Whose car?" Jarques asked.

They both stood there admiring the ride.

"It's mine," Coach said. He ran his hand over the hood.

Jarques said, "Look at the paint on it. It's shining . . . doesn't even look real."

"Chevy Caprice. These are the new cars for detectives."

Jarques walked around the car. "So why do you have it?"

"Hello. I'm a detective now."

Jarques continued to walk around the car without looking up, as if Coach's comment didn't mean a thing. "Look at the tires on this thing. They look like they grip the road like suction cups or something."

Coach hit the unlock button on the key fob. "Wait until you get inside and ride. Unbelievable. Let's go." When Coach started up the car and told Jarques to buckle up, the sound of the engine made them both stop what they were doing and take notice. There was no denying the car's power. Coach pulled away, and Jarques began to look around the car's interior and get comfortable.

"How fast does it go?"

Coach looked at him. "One sixty or so. They told me at the garage that it's a V-eight with three hundred fifty-five horses."

"Dang. What you need to go that fast for?"

Coach hesitated. "Hope I never find out."

Coach realized the excitement of riding in such a beast of a car made it all but impossible for Jarques to discuss proper attire, like he'd planned on doing, so he abandoned that idea and they just enjoyed the ride all the way to their destination.

Coach pulled into the parking lot of Men's Fashions Shop.

"I can tell already that Macy's has more suits than this little place," Jarques said.

"Really?"

"Yeah, this place is extra small."

Jarques found out the shop was small in terms of its dimensions, but Macy's couldn't compare to what he saw inside. There were at least sixty rows of suits, jackets, ties, shoes, pants, and everything in between. Coach didn't have to say a word, because the look of amazement on Jarques's face was enough for him. His tailor, Butch, came over to greet them. He let them know that as soon as they found something they liked, he would be right over to take their measurements.

Jarques said, "Measurements? I'm, like, five feet eleven, Coach."

"Not your height, boy. Your chest, shoulders, neck, sleeves, and waist. You are getting a tailored suit."

"Tailored?"

"Yeah, they're going to size the suit according to your body dimensions so that you'll look like a million dollars."

Jarques looked around at the suits. "I don't really need a suit to look like a million dollars."

"Is that right?"

"Yup," he confirmed with youthful confidence.

Coach said, "Well, what would make you look like a million dollars, J?"

Jarques looked around. "Some True Religion jeans maybe. They got that?"

"They got that? They got that?" Coach repeated.

"Yeah. Do they?"

Coach said, "Hell no, they ain't got that, and speak proper English, okay? This is a men's store that sells men's suits and accessories. Look around. There are no jeans, no T-shirts, and no damn sneakers. The clothing in this store gets you in the door, son."

"What door?"

"The front door of opportunity. The door you'll one day walk through for an interview for a job. You can't walk into an interview with True Religion."

Coach called the tailor over to take their measurements. He was having a good time and believed what he was doing would benefit Jarques in the long run. Looking and speaking like a gentleman would take him much further in life than getting in the habit of throwing on the latest style of jeans. It didn't take the young buck long to begin to understand what getting a tailored suit meant. Coach noticed that Jarques was enjoying himself, looking in all directions in the three-way mirror, as their tailor took his measurements for three suits after tuning the radio to his favorite station. Coach didn't have to persuade Jarques to take a good look at the shoes. Jarques liked two pairs as soon as he laid eyes on them. Coach was relieved the day was going so smoothly. However, when he answered his phone as he walked up to the cashier to pay for their items, all of that seemed to change in an instant.

27

The cashier rang up their items and then told Coach the damage. He gave her his credit card while trying to listen to what was being said by the person on the other end of the line at the same time. He could barely hear anything at all because there were sirens blaring and constant commotion in the background. When the background noise subsided, he finally had a chance to hear what was being said.

"They beat her, Coach. Those bastards beat her."

"Hello? Who is this?"

"It's Theadore!"

"Tall? What's going on? Why all the sirens?"

"Ms. Lois was beaten," he said.

Coach was shocked at the news and wanted to know what had happened.

"She came down to her house to get a few items, and not even fifteen minutes later I came down to see what was keeping her and found her beaten." Mr. Tall paused, and Coach could hear him tell an officer on the scene her last name. "It's bad, Coach. She's real bad. I don't know if she's going to make it."

Coach signed the receipt, got his credit card back, grabbed the bags with their shoes and accessories, and rushed to the car, with Jarques at his side. He made sure Jarques was buckled in his seat nice and tight before he flipped the switches for the siren on the Chevy. As they made their way to the scene, he didn't say much to Jarques. He did glance over at him a few times to make sure he was okay. His mind was focusing on the job and now this case. This was his assigned case now, handed down only the day before. It had taken off in a direction he hadn't imagined it would. He realized that the top brass wanted the break-ins and the threats handled, and he had given Lois his word that he would help find the bastards who were threatening the neighborhood and committing the robberies. And now she was on her way to the hospital.

Jarques held on to the handle above the passenger window when, for the first time, Coach pushed the gas pedal all the way to the floor and they could feel every one of the 355 horses gallop in unison down the open stretch of road.

28

When Coach arrived at the scene, there were about four police cruisers in front of the house. The Georgia Bureau of Investigation vans had arrived and the techs were more than likely inside, dusting the place for fingerprints and taking pictures.

"Aren't you going in?" Jarques said. His eyes were wide and observant.

Coach just sat there and watched the police activity. It seemed as though he was trying to get himself charged up for the next phase of his career, as a detective on the force.

"Yeah. Just taking a moment," he explained.

Jarques said, "Someone dead inside?"

"No."

"Then why all the police cars?"

"Something bad happened inside."

Jarques was full of questions. "You know them or something?"

"Yeah."

"Aren't you going to check it out?"

"I'm going to wait here until Coach Calvin comes to get you and take you back to school. Looks like I'll be here awhile."

"What about practice?"

"Canceled."

"Must be serious?" Jarques said.

"It is," Coach confirmed.

Coach got a burst of adrenaline when he noticed a few cops gather together, exchanging comments. He wanted to rush out and join them, but he didn't want to leave Jarques alone in the car at a crime scene. He sat and wondered what they were talking about. How bad was Ms. Lois? Was she going to make it? Who the fuck had the balls to walk into an elderly woman's house and beat her up? The police force hated this type of shit. Whoever did it was going to get their fuckin' ass beat before they were read their rights. Fuck that.

"I don't know why you even like this job . . . besides this car," Jarques said.

Coach kind of chuckled. It was more like he blew the comment off. He was heated and was ready to go inside. He took out his phone. "I'm helping people, Jarques."

"But you can get killed helping people. Crazy."

Coach thought about the possibility. "Yeah." The phone connected after he dialed.

"Calvin, where are you?"

"Coming right around the corner, man. I got you," Calvin said.

Coach stepped out of the car and waited for Calvin.

Jarques opened the passenger door. The commotion and action here were much better than at the movies. He saw the flashing lights, the quickly moving cops, and that yellow tape around the trees that sectioned off the location of the crime. There were even people standing around, and a few were even crying. Then a television crew pulled up.

Calvin arrived about a minute later. He parked and walked toward Coach, checking out the scene as he went.

"Wow, man, looks like you have a situation up in here," Calvin said. "When I first drove up, I thought all these cops were over at Tall's."

"This is his friend's house," Coach said.

"Lois?"

"Yeah."

"I don't see Tall. Is he all right?"

"Yeah. He went to the hospital with her," Coach informed him.

Calvin looked over at Jarques, and while he and Coach continued to chat, Jarques turned and looked into the crowd of onlookers. He locked eyes with the same group of guys that he had noticed the night he came out of the store with candy while Coach was waiting for him in the car. It was much too late to act as though he didn't see them.

"Hey, take J back to school for me," Coach said

Calvin said, "Yeah, sure, man. No problem. What about practice?"

"Cancel it, Calvin. I know we have a big one coming up, but today it's not going to happen."

"Got you," Calvin said. "I will call you when he walks through the doors."

"Cool," Coach said.

29

Before he went into Ms. Lois's home, now a crime scene, Coach looked over at the neighbors who had gathered around. He scanned their faces because he happened to be facing them as he moved in the direction of the house, not because he found any of them suspicious. After taking two steps into the house, Coach couldn't help but think of Ms. Lois. Her home was a reflection of her feisty character and was updated for its age.

"I thought your ass had taken that car back and switched back into that gotdamned PR gear," the watch commander said from behind.

Coach turned around. "Nah, I'm here."

"I see," he said. "And I see that this is your shit. The shit you were running your mouth about when you were in your community service mode."

Coach was looking around the place and did not glance at his brother in-law. "Yeah, just like I told you. The threats, the crimes of these motherfuckers are real."

"Gotdamn right, they're real. If that old lady makes it, I will know for sure there's a God," he said.

Coach gazed at him hard. He didn't really want to know how bad Lois had been beaten. "Let me get started on this shit, man. I already feel bad enough," he said.

The watch commander began to walk away. "Oh, yeah, you need to hurry your ass up in here."

"Why?"

"Notice of security just came down. Every fuckin' swinging dick and hard nipple is reporting at schools to show our presence."

"Geez, man, for what?" Coach asked.

"Fuckin' shooting this morning in Connecticut. Fuckin' bastard went into a school and shot up some precious babies. Looks like a slaughterhouse, from what I hear."

"School kids?"

"Smallest ones around," he told Coach.

Coach remained quiet and tried to process it all.

The watch commander gave him a moment, then said, "Yeah, I know. Who can talk after news like that? Look, I kept Ben Hill open for you since that's where most of your boys on your team are out of. Let me know when you are on-site." He began to walk away. "Just crazy, man."

Coach thought about it. "Yeah, got it."

Coach pulled his writing pad and pen out of his suit jacket pocket. He already knew the drill of watching his steps and not fucking up evidence. So he just stood close to the door while trying to get a sense of what took place here. He ventured into the living room, where most of the GBI forces were, and that was where he saw the blood, a pool of it, along with a lady's shoe, which was lying near the kitchen entrance. Coach made sure he didn't get in the way as he approached a crime tech who was leaning over a portion of the blood, collecting evidence.

Coach said, "What you got there?"

"Some of her face," the tech said. "Damn ass wipes. Who the hell beats an old woman like this?"

"Did you get a chance to see her before she was taken away?"

"Just a glance. Not good, man."

"What type of chance you give her?"

"Not a chance in hell, if you ask me, but hell, I'm not a doctor, so who knows?"

Coach hesitated, then looked around. "What about some prints? Tell me they left some prints."

"Not one yet. But I got some fiber from that chair over there."

"What is it?"

"Looks like some material from some jeans."

30

Coach went through all the evidence he could at the crime scene. There wasn't much. Not enough to tell who the hell was acting so ill-bred and foul. He had to get over to the school next.

He parked the Chevy in the school parking lot thirty minutes before the students were scheduled to be dismissed. He hadn't heard much about the shooting in Connecticut, so on the way over to the school, he listened to the radio dispatcher relay constant updates to the troops patrolling the streets. There was an announcement over the air to expect higher than normal traffic at the schools, as parents would want to pick up their children on such a terrible day. The quiet time Coach had in the car was good, because it gave him the chance to go over his crime-scene notes and try to get some type of lead on the asshole that went ballistic on Lois.

The back patio door of her home was open when Lois was discovered. Coach figured that was probably the way the punks left, because the neighbors who were outside during the time of the assault didn't see anyone leave through the front door. There were also footprints in the dirt leading from the patio all the way to a fence in the yard, which they must have jumped over to leave unnoticed. The food left on the table and the spilled beer were obvious signs that they had been in the house awhile, and the fact that the bed linens in both bedrooms had been pulled back suggested that they had been there overnight.

Coach was hoping that DNA in the beds would tell them what they needed to know to make an arrest. Coach could hardly stand the fact that they could have been in her home at the same time he was sitting in her driveway.

It was clear from the jump that the guys he was dealing with were a bunch of nasty punks who would get meaner and meaner by the day if they were not stopped. Where they would strike next was a major concern. The fact that they had slept in a house that they did not have keys to and had occupied the home as if it were their own were clear signs of a sense of entitlement and a lack of respect for the law, or for anything else, for that matter. Coach felt the deep distain he had within him for those walking through life with entitlement issues. He was convinced the bastard who had killed his wife and twins was all about that.This was his first case. He had to bring it home. Not many cases that detectives stepped into, especially right off the bat, had a personal connection. He wanted to go into the streets and find the assholes who had a fetish for beating up defenseless women and put them in jail. He knew they were black. He got that much from Mr. Tall the night he rolled up on them in front of Lois's house. He couldn't let that fact hamper his search for them. Or mess with his mind, since he was well aware of the disproportionate number of young black males who were locked up. These bastards without a doubt needed to be locked up, and he was going to do it.

31

Coach didn't know what to expect as he ventured down the hallway of the hospital to see Lois. He'd talked to Mr. Tall a few times since finding out about the crime, but now it was later in the day. It had been hours since he'd heard anything. Mr. Tall had let him know that he was spending most of his time in the sitting area on her floor. When Coach finally reached him, he found him sitting up straight, arms locked together, and sleeping.

As quietly as he possibly could, because there were others in the sitting area, he called out, "Tall." When Mr. Tall didn't stir, Coach repeated himself two or three times.

Mr. Tall finally opened his eyes slowly. He had missed his two afternoon naps and tried to shake off sleep.

"Tall, you all right?" Coach said.

"Yeah, yeah." Then Mr. Tall tried to get up quickly, like he used to. You could hear him grunt too, but of course, he couldn't get up on his feet. "Lois all right?" She had stayed on his mind even in sleep.

Coach put his hand on Mr. Tall's shoulder so he wouldn't try to get up from the couch again. "I'm here to check on her. How long you been out here?"

Mr. Tall said, "Time is it?"

"Close to seven."

"Seven? You should still be at practice."

"Canceled. I'm on the job."

"Last time I checked on her, she was asleep. Nurse told me that they wanted to run some test." He sat up so far that he was leaning forward with his hands folded. "So, that coffee for me, or you drinking both of 'em?"

Coach had almost forgotten about the coffees as he stood with them in a carrier in his left hand. He looked at them. "One or two sugars?"

Mr. Tall thought for a moment. "Fuck it. Give me two. The way things are going, maybe I'll pass out and die then I won't have to worry about all this shit."

Coach extended the coffee with two sugars, then changed his mind and gave him the cup with one. "Here. Drink this. It'll be okay."

They sat for a while, putting the coffee down when news of the school shooting in Connecticut played on the TV, catching their attention.

"What the hell is going on?" Mr. Tall said. "People today have lost it, Coach, lost all their marbles, man, every last one."

Coach understood well enough. It was hard to stomach. He had noticed the looks on the parents' faces when they picked up their kids at the school today. They had all looked so frightened, as though the shooting had taken place at their school.

"It's just these past twenty years or so, right?" Mr. Tall tried to remember when school shootings became commonplace as he went back into his coffee. "I mean, this here . . ." He pointed to the television screen. "It's too sick for even a sick person to think of. Kids stabbing babies and thugs beating seventy-year-old women without blinking. Real animals must be looking at us, stumped out of their fuckin' minds."

Mr. Tall was right. Things were getting out of hand. They both sat there quietly for a time. A nurse sitting on the other side of the room, watching the television, started crying uncontrollably, giving voice to what they were feeling inside.

"So how is Lois?" Coach said.

Mr. Tall shook his head, looking down at his coffee. "She's bad, man. I don't know how that little, precious woman took all that."

"Talking any?"

"Broken jaw. But she's writing some."

Coach was very interested in that bit of information. He sat up a bit. Hoping. "Did she see who it was?"

"They had on masks, but she says it was them."

"How?"

"They admitted it while they beat her."

"How?"

"Told her, 'Didn't I tell you, I would beat you like a slave?'"

32

After a twenty-minute solemn, glum visit with Lois, Coach and Mr. Tall left her room. There wasn't much to say after seeing her like that. Mr. Tall stood in the hallway, searching for an understanding of her condition. Coach leaned against the wall with his hands in his pockets.

Coach said, "Strong woman in there, man." He thought about all the pounding and pain she had endured. "Strong all the way through, Tall," he added. Coach had been staring at the hospital floor, and when he looked up, he saw that Mr. Tall was in a daze. "Tall?"

Mr. Tall looked up. Coach sensed that Mr. Tall had aged another ten years with all the lack of sleep and worry.

"You know, I've never been married," Mr. Tall said.

Coach listened, without saying a word.

"Sometimes it takes people a little longer to do things than most." Mr. Tall tried to chuckle at his thoughts and did barely.

"Yeah . . ." Coach cosigned, not knowing where the conversation was going.

"I really like that woman in there, Coach. Have for a long time now. You know, sometimes things grow on you and you begin to get used to them, and that's how me and Lois are."

Coach smiled.

"She wasn't married, either, and I would see her sometimes coming home from work, right after I would return from work. She'd either be doing some yard work or sipping on something ice cold right on her porch, watching all the little kids play on our street. Sometimes, she would have the kids from her class over on the weekends to give the parents a break because she could only imagine how hard it was to bring kids up while being married. People need to spend time with one another. She did that, you know?"

Coach said, "That's nice, Tall. I bet it was appreciated."

He thought for a moment. "Yeah, it was. It was. But not enough, not enough to where they would come back a few times or even once a year after the kids had grown and gone to college just to say, 'Thank you' and 'I'm thinking about you.'"

"People not people anymore," Coach mused.

"You're right. They're not like people should be." Mr. Tall paused, then added, "I'm saying all this because I would thank Lois all the time."

"Yeah?"

"Oh, yeah. Thank her for what she did, 'cause I could see it from afar. Thank her for being the type of woman who I never, ever seen have a bunch of mess around her— what you youngins call drama—all around her home. She didn't want any of that." Mr. Tall managed a brief smile. "I'd thank her for dealing with those kids every day and treating every last one like they were her own. I would even stop her car when she was on her way home if I'd see her while checking my mail, and I'd just thank her for always smiling when she saw me—every time, Coach. Every time."

"Yeah, that's real people right there," Coach said.

Mr. Tall looked into her room. "She was so real that I was going to ask her to marry me."

"Marry?"

"Sure was. During that barbecue we were about to have. I don't have much to lose at this stage in the game. Think it could have worked too. You know why, Coach?"

Coach shook his head no. "Uh-uh. Tell me."

"'Cause we like each other. We genuinely like each other, and when you do that, there are endless opportunities, way beyond the imagination, that can join people together."

Mr. Tall was not hesitant when he informed Coach that he planned on finding out if Lois wanted to marry him. Mr. Tall said he felt bad that he didn't go down to the house with her to get the food out the freezer. He said he felt even worse that while she took that beating, there was nothing he could do for her. He said that he realized he could be there for her now and that he was going to stay next to her side as long as it took. Mr. Tall gave Coach the key to his home and asked if he could go to his house and turn on his porch lights.

It took Coach only a few minutes to go inside Mr. Tall's home to turn on the lights for him. On the way out he noticed a police cruiser sitting in Lois's driveway. He drove down there and found a cop leaning back on the hood of his car.

"Craft," Coach called out when he recognized the officer.

"What's up, Coach?" the officer shot back. "I heard this was your case."

"Yeah, all mine, bruh. Quiet around here or what?"

Craft looked around. "No doubt. I had a few lookyloos come by before darkness because they heard about what happened. But other than that, nobody better bring they ass over here tonight, because I'm not asking any questions, only talking with this sidearm," he replied.

"Yeah . . ." Coach agreed.

"Some things you just don't do, man," Craft said. "This right here is why I am police. I'm telling you, I hope I don't run into who did this, and I'm not alone. Everyone in this sector is pissed. Let me put it like this. Whoever did it better be living in a fuckin' cave, man."

Coach looked toward the house. "Look, I'm going to go in. See if I missed anything earlier."

"Take your time. I'm here all night," Craft told him.

The door was unlocked. Coach walked in. He paused for a brief second when he first heard the fragments of broken glass and other items cracking and popping under his shoes. What a mess. So many broken items lay on the floor in the house. Shit had been thrown everywhere. Coach estimated that Lois had lain just a half inch from where the huge 100 percent oak cabinet that stood along the length of her wall had been thrown to the floor. Those bastards really did try to kill her. He could see blood from one end of the room to the spot where she was found. They had dragged her there, hoping the cabinet would fall on top of her.

Coach had to take a deep breath to prevent himself from getting too emotional while he tried to piece together in his mind what had taken place here. He had a seat in the same chair that one of the punks had sat in when Lois encountered them. He wondered if they had sat there. Coach looked around and remembered he had had the entire kitchen table checked for fingerprints. He took out his phone and called the lab and learned that so far, no prints had come back that identified who the bastards were. This wasn't going to be easy.

Coach sat still for almost an hour, scanning every bit of the room, looking for something, anything, until his eyes focused on a picture that had fallen to the floor. The picture was in a broken glass frame. It was so close to the chair that all he had to do was reach down and pick it up. The picture was titled "Third Grade Class." All the children in the photo were standing and had bright smiles on their faces. They had no idea of their future, but they looked happy, as though recess was next on the agenda for them all. A little girl with pigtails stood out to him. It was her smile. She was holding Lois's hand. In a million years Coach would never forget this smile. It had followed her throughout her life. He searched for her name in the list below the photo to make sure. It was her. The smiling child happened to be his wife as a little girl.

33

Coach didn't have the courage to even attempt to be alone that night. It had been an up-and-down day, one that had started on a good note with getting suits with Jarques but had devolved into finding out Lois had been beaten, visiting her in the hospital, witnessing Mr. Tall's pain, and seeing his dead wife as a little girl with the same smile she would show him every day that he knew her.

Shonda picked up her cell phone on the first ring, and she told Coach that she had been sitting there waiting for his call.

"I can't be alone tonight," Coach told her.

Shonda said, "Bad day, huh?"

"One like never before."

"Wish I could come over to keep you company," she said. "No way I can leave Jarques here alone, though."

"And I would never ask you to," he said back. "By the way, I'm in your driveway."

"Are you serious?"

"I have my things. I need to be with you tonight."

Within seconds, Shonda flicked on the porch light, opened the front door, and said into the phone while looking directly at Coach, who was still sitting in his car, "Well, c'mon in. You're always welcome here."

Coach climbed out of the car and followed Shonda inside the house.

Shonda sat down on the couch with Coach and poured two glasses of wine. "Believe it or not, this is a three-dollar bottle of wine," she said.

Coach looked at the bottle, then took a sip. "Um, pretty good. Thanks. I really need it."

"I got you, old man. . . ."

"We're not that much older than one another. Fourteen years apart."

"Believe me, fourteen years is a long time."

"If you say so."

"I do." Then she kissed him on the cheek.

He looked around. "J asleep?"

"He should be. Said he was tired. I had him put on those shirts you got him. I think he really likes them."

"Really?"

"Yeah, he even showed me how to tie his tie."

Coach smiled. "That's good. I learned something today too."

She said, "From Jarques?"

"Yeah. He told me all about the True Religion brand."

She laughed at the thought.

"Sure did. Told me it's what he needs to look good."

"These kids have been brainwashed. I'm glad you didn't bring any True Religion up in here. What he has is just fine." Shonda observed Coach for a moment. "First day on the job and you're already bringing it home with you, aren't you?"

Coach said, "Can't help it on this one. Too personal."

"Remember, we can only control ourselves, so try not to let it get you down, okay?"

"Thank you," he said. "Always good to hear someone with a level head."

Shonda smiled at him. "I'm here."

"Mean that?"

She nodded her head yes.

Coach said, "Well, if that's the case, we need to make it official."

"Make *what* official?"

He pointed at her, then back at himself. This . . . you, me . . . as in one."

"Are you serious?"

"I mean, only if you want to. I don't want to have to twist your arm to be with a brother."

"Twist my arm? You would never have to do that."

"Okay, cool, then. We're going to do this. We are officially dating."

Shonda hit him on the leg. "See? You are an old man, with all this official stuff."

34

The next morning Coach was well rested. He was more than ready to find the idiot deviants who had beat Lois and to put them behind bars. He offered Jarques a ride to school, and the boy accepted. This time, though, their ride together was odd. Odd because Shonda had revealed to Jarques that she and Coach were now an item. Neither Coach nor Jarques knew how to start the first conversation. This day was a fresh start for their relationship too.

They were maybe a few minutes from the house when Jarques said, "I see you stayed the night."

Coach was sort of hesitant. "Yeah. Yeah, sure did," he said.

"Was everything okay?"

Coach turned to him quickly. "Excuse me?"

"With our place, Coach. Did you sleep okay?"

"Yeah, yeah, I did. Thanks."

Jarques said, "You know, my mom must really like you."

"Oh, really?"

Jarques smiled and waited awhile before he explained. "Yeah, it's been weeks since the last guy stayed over."

Coach took his eyes off the road and looked at Jarques.

"Relax, man. Just teasing," Jarques said.

"What about you?"

"Me?"

"Yeah, you have a girlfriend?"

Coach had never noticed Jarques smile so wide before. It was the first time he had even had a really good look at the blue braces in the boy's mouth. "Yeah, I got a few . . ." He sat up straight.

"A few?"

"Yeah, you know."

"How they feel about that?"

Jarques laughed. "I don't know. I mean, what can they do? It's just like that these days."

"Oh, it's like that?"

"Yeah, it's just like that." Jarques noticed Coach move his head from side to side. "What?"

"Nothing. It's cool. It's cool."

Jarques leaned forward. "Hey, this is cool right here. That's my boy right there. I'll walk in with him."

Coach stopped the car and watched Jarques climb out and walk toward the school grounds with his friend. Coach easily recalled his days as a young buck without a care in the world as he drove toward the department to get his day started.

Lois's house was still being watched by rolling patrol cars throughout the day, and earlier in the day Coach made sure he went to Mr. Tall's and turned off his lights. He had spoken with Mr. Tall about an hour before lunch and had learned that Lois was still in and out of consciousness, but her doctor was impressed because her vitals were getting stronger, which made everyone feel much better. Mr. Tall had insisted that he needed to get a walk in and stretch his legs, or he was going to explode from so much stress, so he asked Calvin to pick him up from the hospital and take a walk with him for an hour or so in order for him to get his blood circulating.

Even though he was on the desk for almost three years, Coach had always kept in touch with his contacts. It seemed as though he'd become closer to them over the three years, because most of the time when he'd reached out to them, it was just to see how they were doing. They would be a big help when he needed information.

One of his favorite informants was Lester. Lester James was the most talented athlete Coach had ever seen who didn't have the intangibles to become great and to use his ability to carve a better life for himself. Coach met Lester his senior year of high school as he coached Lester's little brother, who was attempting to follow in his big brother's footsteps. Lester had been a beast on the football field from eighth grade all the way up to his senior year, when his friends helped him decide that he would be an even bigger beast on the streets, committing crimes, which meant an end to anything else he wanted to do with his life.

Lester had been Coach's informant ever since Coach had helped him out after other beat cops found crack in his pockets, which he was trying to sell. For no other reason other than the fact that he was coaching Lester's little brother, Coach talked the cops into letting him handle the situation, and from that point on Lester had been forthcoming with any information Coach needed.

Lester had also done right by Coach, and deep down he'd always be grateful to him.

When Coach received the call that his wife had been killed in a car accident, he and Lester had been meeting at a park and Lester had been filling Coach in on a low-level drug dealer. Coach was in shock after receiving the call, and Lester put him in his police cruiser and drove him home, then sat outside on his front porch until someone came to take care of him. They had only spoken by phone in the past three years, but Coach knew if he wanted to get some information and quick, Lester could get it, so he called him and they agreed to meet at the Pancake House.

"I remember a time when this place would have a line wrapped around the building," Lester said.

"That's when the food was good," Coach said.

Lester was looking around the establishment almost like he was scared to put his elbows on the table, even though he looked like shit himself. "Yeah, it does look a little dusty up in this bitch. You should arrest them or some shit." Lester checked out his coffee mug for cleanliness before he took a sip.

"So, how you doin', man?" Coach asked him.

Lester said, "You know, I'm making it. That alone is something of a good thing these days. You know what I mean?"

"Yeah, I know. And li'l bro? What's up with him these days?"

Lester smiled. "College grad. He finished playing at Eastern Oregon, and now he's an engineer with a wife and a son of his own in Portland."

Coach smiled too. "See? That's what the hell I'm talking about. Have to share that with my team after practice today."

"You still coaching?"

"Of course. I would have too much time on my hands if I didn't."

"Plus, you enjoy it. I know you do. Even remember when you would give advice when I was in high school." Lester looked off into space. "My black ass should have listen too."

Coach didn't know what to say, because he knew he'd been right, but he wasn't going to pile on. Instead, he said, "Look, Lester, I really appreciate what you did the day of the accident."

"Oh, that? Look, not a problem. I mean, what was I going to do? Leave you there?" Lester has done a lot of shit in his life, but when a man is down, one thing I can say about Lester is that I've always helped him up . . . unless I'm the motherfucker that put him down," he said. His laughter was in remembrance of his dirty deeds. And Coach noticed that he looked around and checked out his back a few times in a protective kind of way.

Coach pushed his plate away after taking one bite of his food. "I can't eat this, man."

"Told you not to order that shit, bruh."

Coach drank some water. "Look, I have an elderly woman who was beaten up a few days ago in her house. You heard about any crews running buck wild about that?"

Lester thought about it for a few moments, then sighed. "Man, these streets have changed since you were in uniform, and that's what? Damn near three, four years ago?"

"Yeah, yeah," Coach said. He took a few seconds and reflected on the fact that so much had changed in such a short time.

Lester said, "There are so many different crews now. So many that an old head like me just tries to survive and keep my ass away from these crazy little motherfuckers. These days you got boys who want to do right, and the rest don't give a damn about anything but taking."

Coach said, "These guys here, I think these are the same ones behind all the home robberies out there."

Lester said, "Heard about it. You know Mom and them don't talk to me that much anymore, but when their shit was broken into, you know I was the first one they thought of," he said, shaking his head before getting some water. "They still treat me like a crackhead, man, and I ain't never taken a hit of that shit. I just sold it."

"Family man, what ya goin' to do?" Coach said. It reminded him to call and check on his family up east.

"You're right. You're right. But I haven't heard about any crews that have been taking it to the elderly, man. I mean, that right there is a no-no. You see . . . most of these boys try to get a reputation by jumping into shit they have no business being in and roughing people up who don't want to move out of the way. The only thing I've heard of is knuckleheads walking up to people and just knocking them the fuck out for the thrill of it. Some knockout game or something."

Coach said, "Nah, the punks I'm looking for are on some retaliation with her because she wanted to know why they were always walking her block, looking into houses and whatnot."

Lester thought for a moment. "The other day in the shop I heard some guys speaking about some thugs who have been waiting outside of a check-cashing joint for people to cash their checks. They make people cash their check and hand over the cash as soon as they walk out or take one in the head," Lester told him. "They were even talking about how these dudes run up in high school girls' homes and dare their daddies to say a word about it." Coach listened intently. "These are not young cats, though who should be in high school or something. These guys are older. Old enough to know better. I don't have a name or location on them, but if it comes up, I will give you a call."

35

The only thing worse than a crime was not finding out who committed it. The fact that he had no lead in his first case as a detective, and that the crime had been carried out against someone he knew personally, was not sitting well with Coach. He was beginning to exhibit a real lack of patience. At this point, Coach didn't care. After Mr. Tall informed him that the local television station was there at the hospital to speak with Lois about her ordeal, Coach filled the Chevy up with gas and hit the streets of the community to find the bastards who did it, because once the interview aired, everyone would be on alert and the whole neighborhood would be uneasy if these fools hadn't been found. Members of the community would know through the media that they needed to take precautions, but the assholes who beat up Lois needed a wake-up call as well, and Coach decided to give them one.

Coach had kind of forgotten that there were so many people walking around on the streets in the middle of the day. Maybe there were more than he remembered. His desk job had given him a sort of closed-captioned view of the world. He decided that maybe the unemployment rate was responsible for the number of people walking around. But he didn't give a damn. Every person whom he rolled up on was getting questioned, and if they had a problem with it, they could call his boss, and he never returned calls.

Coach drove past Lois's house again. As he passed her house, he caught sight of a young man in a hoodie, walking along with his hands in his pockets. Coach slowed down, matching the speed of the young man on foot. When he acted like he didn't see him in the car, Coach hit the whistle. The young man stopped and turned and looked at Coach through the tinted windows.

"What?" he yelled out as he turned his palms toward the sky.

Coach stopped the car, got out and walked over to him. "What you mean, what? You better show me some respect."

He was silent.

"What's your name?" Coach said.

"Why?"

"'Cause I asked."

"I don't have to tell you nothing," he said.

Coach looked around. "Look, I'm about to smack your ass, son. Now, what's your name?"

"Mac."

"Take off that hood, Mac. I need to see your face."

Coach could tell he was about to give him some more of that mouth, so he shook his head no.

Mac just did what he said and kept quiet.

"Where you headed?" Coach said.

"Home."

"Where is home?"

"It is where it is. I'm not telling you shit."

Coach could not believe the attitude this guy had. He was young, about twenty-three, but he couldn't be ignorant about the fact that he should keep his mouth shut and show some respect to his elders, especially the police. Coach moved closer to him.

"Do you beat up old ladies, Mac?"

"What?" he said. He looked at Coach, very puzzled.

"I said . . . Do you hit on old ladies?"

Mac stepped back. "Fuck you talking about, man?"

"Just what I said. I am looking for someone who beat up an old lady and left her for dead. Do you know anybody who would do that?"

"Nah, man. What you asking me for?"

"'Cause you're here and I need to know."

"Well, no. I didn't do it and don't know who did."

Coach stood there and stared at him for a while, then turned to go back to the car.

Mac mumbled, "You're just pulling people off the street and asking stupid-ass questions. What you need to do is go over a few blocks and see why everybody in that check-cashing place ain't coming out with no money."

Coach had his hand on the car door by this point, but he froze and looked at Mac. "Say what?" Twice in the same day he had heard about this check-cashing mess.

Mac looked around, hesitated. He put the hood of his hoodie back over his head and looked around again. "Those motherfuckers in the check-cashing joint, they in there waiting for people to cash their checks, and then they take the money. Every dime of it."

Coach said, "They get you, Mac? Is that why you're walking around out here pissed at the world?"

"They ain't get me, not today at least. Last week, though, they took the money I made mowing and cleaning up at the corner store. I just saw them inside from across the street. Forget that I need my money. I'll go to the grocery store and cash my check." Mac started to walk away.

Coach called out, "Hey, c'mon. I'll take you anyplace you need to be."

Mac looked at Coach, then looked around and thought about it. "Fuck you, man."

36

Coach wanted to look into Mac's claims. It definitely sounded like some entitlement immorality was popping off. He drove the two blocks over to the check-cashing center. He parked in a wide parking lot, in between two cars so that he wouldn't be seen. Coach had always detested these downtrodden places. Made the whole neighborhood look like a dump or like a cheese line, which he knew too much about while growing up. It could at least look like a place of business. Coach could go to the other side of town and never see one of these oppressive places. It looked like a shack and blended in nicely with all the other demoralizing businesses in the hood. Car-rim huts, nail salons, hair salons, and horrid package stores with the nervous bootleg video salesman peeking around the corner, whispering, "Hey, bruh."

Once he was looking inside his target from his spot in the parking lot, he realized how nice the triple-tinted windows were on his car. No sun could get in, and no one could see in. As far as he could see through the shop window, there were a few people in line, with their backs to him. And he could just make out a white man behind the counter. Coach thought about going into the joint and just turning it upside down, but he knew he needed to be patient. After about thirty minutes or so he had watched a few people go in, come out, and just continue on their way without incident.

After about forty-five minutes things slowed down a bit. Coach was about to call it a wrap, but then a black Impala pulled up and two black males who looked to be in their twenties came out the door, quickly got in the car, and drove off. Coach hadn't seen them go in the joint and figured they'd been inside all this time. A few minutes later, just as Coach was going to follow the Impala, an older white man flipped a sign that said OUT TO LUNCH on the inside of the door to the place, came out, locked the door, walked to his car, an old black Volvo station wagon, and then drove off.

Coach decided to follow him instead. After about four minutes Coach turned on the blaring siren and the flashers on his car and pulled the man over to the side of the road. When he was approaching the man's vehicle, Coach could see him looking in his rearview mirror, and that was when he realized the white man had a gray goatee and red hair. Coach stood still as the man rolled down his window.

"I'm confused. You're not street police," the man said.

Coach waited a few beats to answer him because he had to take a look in the backseat. He noticed newspapers, magazines, and a dog chain there. On the passenger seat up front he saw a money bag. "No need for the confusion. You're right," Coach said.

The driver said, "So, what do you want?" His words rushed out, and he looked ahead at the road instead of at Coach.

Coach said, "We'll get to that in a minute. What's your name?"

He said, "Harry. You know what? Fuck this. . . . Can I see your ID?" Harry still hadn't looked Coach in the eye. He just put his hand out the window, waiting for Coach to give him the ID.

Coach smiled and gave him five and said, "Show me yours first, Harry."

Harry didn't like it, and the frown on his face told Coach as much. Harry dug into his pocket, pulled out his wallet, withdrew his license, and let Coach see it.

Coach had said, "Harry Henry, huh? McDonough, Georgia . . . sixty-six years old and five feet four." Coach gave him an investigative look. "It says your hair is gray, Harry?"

Harry finally looked at Coach. Then he ran his hand through his hair. "Oh, this. My teenage daughters thought I would be cool with the red hair," he told Coach.

Coach said, "I see."

Harry's tone changed. "I still haven't seen your ID, bud."

Coach took out his ID, flashed it at Harry, and without hesitation pushed himself up against Harry's door, getting up close and personal. "Look, asshole. I know you got thugs in your place of business, robbing people right in front of you."

Harry's eyes widened, but he didn't say a word.

Coach told him, "Don't tell me you don't, because I have a witness who says you do."

This guy Harry was quick to offer up some details. "Look, okay, I didn't set this up. These guys are ruthless. They came to me with this. I mean, I know it's wrong, but nobody's complained yet."

"Are you kidding me, Harry?" Coach said.

"What'd I say?"

Coach said, "I should take you in right now." Coach noticed Harry grab the steering wheel. Coach said, "Take the keys out of the ignition and put them on the seat."

Harry removed the keys and placed them on the money bag.

"So, tell me, how do these guys take this money without anyone going to the police?"

Harry said, "They're probably scared, and the fact that they tell them that they will kill their whole family . . ."

"Just a threat, huh?"

"That's all it takes. It's like they have some type of reputation that scares people," he said. "I don't know and I don't ask."

"How much do you get out of this?"

"I get to live, damn it. Look, I'm too old for prison. I have daughters, no mother. All I do is what they tell me. When they are inside with me and a customer cashes a check, they take it all."

Coach waited for a few cars to pass them. "Names? You have names for me? Whose car did they jump in, and where are they going?"

"Man, you're going to get me killed."

"Rather die in prison?"

"Vernon and Mark, real mean assholes," he said. "I don't know who picked them up or where they are going, and I could care less."

"Guns on them?"

"Haven't seen any. They usually slap people around if they talk back. But to be so bold, I would guess, yeah, they do. The guy Vernon, he's the mean one. He takes the money, puts it in his pocket, and doesn't count it until he leaves."

"Where can I find them?"

"I don't know. They never say. All they ever tell me is when they're coming back."

Coach didn't take his eyes off of Harry, because he had a feeling he was lying.

"Later today," Harry told him. "They said they would be back later."

37

The scumbags that Coach saw drive away from Harry's place of business—Vernon, Mark, and Chucky—were all sitting in the Impala across from a bank. Chucky was at the wheel, and they were all quiet, waiting and watching.

Chucky said, "So what are we waiting for outside this bank?"

Vernon was in the backseat. He said, "We're going to rob it."

Mark smiled.

"Bull . . . shit," Chucky said. "Fuck you and that."

Mark was in the front with Chucky, and he began to laugh with Vernon.

Chucky said, "I'm serious. Why did you have me pick you up and drive out here?"

"'Cause I did," Vernon said. "What? You have another interview or some craziness like that?"

"Oh, yeah . . . did you get the job or what?" Mark asked.

Chucky thought about his question and looked out the window, in a daze. "Nah." But he knew these two were messing with him and didn't care if he did or not.

Vernon and Mark laughed again.

Vernon said, "Tried to tell your ass. They are not hiring black men these days. Don't you know the unemployment rate has never been higher for a black man?"

Mark said, "I can't lie. You did try to tell him."

"Man . . . forget y'all," Chucky mumbled.

Vernon said, "Don't worry about it, though. We 'bout to get paid."

"Damn right," Mark said.

"Doing what? Hey, man, don't have me out here, and you're about to do something stupid," Chucky said.

Vernon hesitated, then looked at Chucky. "Tell me something. How come when I know a way we can get some money, it's stupid, but your way of getting money is so damn noble?"

"Because it's the right way to do it."

"Says you. If you must know, we're sitting here because I want to make sure this is Harry's bank," Vernon said.

Chucky said, "Who the hell is Harry?"

"The old dude who has the spot we just came from," Mark said.

"I want to make sure this is his bank because if it is, he's going to be writing me a check for everything in his account," Vernon said. "He practically runs a bank, so he has to have money."

"And what would make you think he would just give you a check?" Chucky said.

Vernon pulled out a pistol and moved closer to the front seat and showed it to Chucky.

Chucky hated messing around with these two so much. He looked around and made sure they couldn't be seen. "Hey, put that up. Out here in my car, carrying pistols and whatnot. Don't you know that's a mandatory ten years in the state?"

Mark said, "Well, you better not tell anybody."

Mark and Vernon were enjoying their comic show.

Vernon said, "Mark, keep an eye out for his car. Knowing Harry, he's going to walk that money bag in there himself. Such a stingy man."

"Look, I don't appreciate this shit, man. You called me to give you a ride home. Not this shit," Chucky said.

"Too bad. We're here now," Vernon said.

Chucky said, "Forget this. I'm leaving. Got guns and shit in my car."

"No, you're not," Vernon said.

Chucky didn't give a care about what Vernon said. He started his car.

Mark pointed to the bank. "Look, there he is, walking it in."

"Just like I thought. Let's go," Vernon said.

38

Coach warned Harry that if he told Vernon or Mark that he had spoken to him, Coach would put him in jail for the rest of his life. He told him he would also close up his irritating shop, which kept the people in the community in a bind. Coach took down Harry's number and let him go to lunch and deposit his money bag. Coach didn't know what his plan was right off, but he knew that since these guys were bold enough to just take hard-earned cash right out the hands of people, then they might know who was behind the assault of Lois, which was his most pressing piece of business.

As Coach waited for Vernon and Mark to return to the shop, he made three phone calls. One to Shonda, one to Mr. Tall, and one to Calvin. The call to Calvin concerned practice and the practice plan. Coach said that the team looked out of shape, and at practice he wanted to run them up and down the field in a no-huddle offense to work on plays and conditioning at the same time. Calvin said that he agreed but wanted to make sure his defense was on the field too, because he knew the team they were playing next ran the exact offense from time to time.

The phone call to Mr. Tall was to check in and see how Lois was doing. Mr. Tall hadn't been home yet, and Coach was still going back and forth to his home, turning the porch light off and on and getting Mr. Tall some clothes too. Mr. Tall said that Lois was getting stronger than ever and was poised to make a full recovery. There was a message on his phone too. It was from Shonda. She wanted to make sure Coach was staying the night again. When Coach called her back, he had to leave a message telling her that he would.

Coach spent the entire afternoon sitting in the parking lot, looking over at the check-cashing enterprise. Around five o'clock the traffic began to pick up on the street. Coach had only an hour before he needed to be at practice. He called Harry, who was inside the shop. Harry let him know that he was closing up shop in five minutes and that the hard ankles that had commandeered his shop had not been in contact with him. No sooner than Coach had put down his phone and prepared to start up the Chevy he noticed the black Impala pull up. One of the guys who he'd seen around lunchtime jumped out and went in to see Harry. The Impala took off as soon as he shut the door.

Coach had planned to take both assholes downtown to question them once he saw them again. But only one went into the shop. He would have to do for now. Coach was antsy. He'd grown tired of waiting for these bums to show up again. He decided without any deliberation that he was going in. He pulled out his Glock nine millimeter and made sure it was fully loaded. He took a deep breath, which had always been his routine when danger was in his path, and looked up into the sky, drawing the sign of the cross on his chest for divine protection. He put his handcuffs at the ready position. Coach had on a hoodie under his leather jacket, and for shits and grins, he pulled the hood of the hoodie over his head, then checked himself out in the rearview mirror before he took the short walk to the shop.

The punk inside was talking to Harry across the counter when Coach walked in. A fucking bell rang when Coach opened the door, as if he was in some sort of freaking grocery mart.

The sound made Harry and his friend look at him, wondering what he wanted. Without any hesitation at all Coach took out his cuffs, and before Harry or his friend could say one word, Coach simultaneously yelled, "Police!" slammed the cuffs on one wrist of his target, pushed his face into the countertop, and then put on the second bracelet, squeezing it nice and tight, over the sound of a bitch-ass scream.

39

Coach needed to unwind after the arrest. After he locked the bracelets on the dog dump who happened to be Vernon and threw him in the car, then placed him in a cell down at the station, he searched for a release. His competitive juices and energy were flowing. So he went head-to-head with Calvin, offense against defense, for the entire practice. After they dismissed the team, Calvin noticed that Coach had a sharp eye on Jarques and Shonda as they walked to the car.

Calvin cleared his throat. "J sure is coming into his own."

Coach turned in Calvin's direction. "Yeah, man, he's getting stronger by the day."

"Looks like this is one of those times when a kid is going to excel when Coach and Mommy get together," Calvin said.

Coach said, "See, right now, I don't know if you're being sarcastic or what."

Calvin smiled. "A little bit, man. You know I have to rub your nose in it after all the bashing you gave me over the years. So everything good?"

"So far," Coach said.

"I can see that."

"What do you mean?"

"You just seem more relaxed, man, when she's around. Seems like you are beginning to let go and continue to live your life." Calvin was fully aware of Coach's loss.

Coach didn't respond, just thought about his friend's words.

Calvin said, "Not to say I would have done it any quicker or even at all. Just saying that you have and I'm glad to see it, brother, and I mean that."

"Thanks."

"So, tell me, what are her friends like? A woman like that must run around in a pack of like minds."

"What?"

"Her friends, Coach. When are you going to have a party or something so you can hook a brother up?"

"Hook a brother up?"

"That's right."

"I don't know, Calvin. But when we do, I will make sure you get that invite, okay?"

After a quick shower at his place and a brief look at the mail, Coach was back at the station, walking through the hall, on his way to question the man who he now knew as Vernon Wise, a twenty-three-year-old transplant from Newark, New Jersey. Coach had called ahead to have him placed in the interrogation room. Right before Coach went in, the watch commander called out to him.

"Finally got him off chill mode, I see."

Coach said, "Yeah. I'm going in now. I don't know if he has anything to do with the assault on Lois Gregory, but I know for damn sure he's been robbing people inside the check-cashing joint."

"Deal making?" the watch commander asked.

"If I have to," Coach said.

"You know, I haven't had a bite of one of these in quite some time, brother in-law."

Coach smiled, then said, "Have some?"

"Don't mind if I do."

The two walked in together, and it took Vernon exactly two seconds after the interrogation room door was shut to confirm to them what kind of a dirtbag he was.

"You motherfuckers just better turn around, go open the front door, and get ready to watch me walk outta here, because I'm not telling you shit." Vernon's hands were handcuffed to the table, and they could see that he was trying in vain to get comfortable in his chair.

Coach said, "Vernon? Vernon . . .Vernon. I bet your mama didn't plan on having you end up in here with a name like Vernon, now did she?"

The watch commander added, "I wouldn't think so. He's not rough enough for this, you son of a bitch."

"Oh, he's not rough. That's why he beats up on old ladies," Coach said. "He's a punk from New Jersey too."

"Yeah, okay. Now I get your drift," the watch commander said. "Yeah, that's a bitch-ass move to beat up an old lady. I'll say this, though. They really like those who participate in bitch-ass moves in state lockup. Hell, even downstairs," he noted.

Vernon sat up in his seat. "Look, I don't know nothing about whatever you're talking about. I do know you ain't got nothing on me and you better let me outta here."

Coach had already sat in the chair across from Vernon, but he stood up from the chair, and as it hit the floor, he was in Vernon's face. "Or what? Or what, gotdamn it? What are you going to do, Vernon, if I don't let you out?"

Vernon looked over at the watch commander. "Yo, man, you better come get your boy."

The watch commander very quietly said, "Or what, Vernon?"

Coach didn't back down. "Little different now, huh, Vernon? Bet if I was an old lady, you would hit me, wouldn't you?"

"Yo, man, I don't know what you're talking about."

"Lois Gregory, that's who I'm talking about. The lady that you beat and left for dead."

Vernon said, "Hey, look here. I didn't beat anybody. Oh, hell no."

The watch commander said, "Where were you on the seventh of this month?"

"Don't matter where I was. I can tell you this. I wasn't nowhere near an old woman. You got me twisted, yo."

Coach walked away from him. "Well, if you can't tell me where you were, shit . . . you're going to be up in here for a long time."

"And we got plenty of room," the watch commander added.

Vernon looked around, as if weighing his options. "Look, I was probably out doing what I do."

"Which is what?" the watch commander said.

"Out, man, riding around. Out."

Coach was standing with his back to Vernon. "Out plotting, trying to figure out how to take something that doesn't belong to you? Is that what you mean?"

Vernon thought about it for a while. "Well, yeah, that sounds like me. I tell you what, though. I didn't beat up any damn woman, I can tell you that."

"Do you know who did?" the watch commander asked.

"No, hell no, man."

Coach turned around and looked at Vernon more closely. "Wait a minute. I know you."

"You don't know me," Vernon told him.

Coach picked his chair up off the floor. He sat down across from Vernon. "Yeah . . . I do know you." Coach pointed at him. "You're that slimeball, son of a bitch nut that was kicked out of Stonecrest Park because you and hundreds of others were betting on the youth football games."

Vernon didn't deny or confirm Coach's assertion. He just stared at Coach, as if he was trying to place him.

Coach looked at his watch commander. "This guy has no shame in his game and will do anything to make a buck. This broomstick bet on Little League football, and then he got kicked out of the park. Can never return. What you did made national headlines. Had sports news agencies all on your sorry ass."

Vernon was silent and looked away.

There was a knock on the door of the interrogation room. The watch commander opened it, and he was handed a Polaroid camera. He shut the door and began to fiddle with the camera.

Coach started to mess with Vernon. Blow his head up a bit. This tactic usually worked on punks who wouldn't admit to anything. Made them feel like somebody walked around, talking about their asses like they were running things. Coach said, "Supposedly, everything that happens on this side of town, you know about. I mean, that's what I hear. I thought about that and thought it was all bullshit, though, not only because your name is Vernon, but who would be scared of you, yo? Huh? Tell me."

"You just have to ask them," he said.

"Them?"

The watch commander leaned across the table so that he was right in front of Vernon. "Smile, motherfucka." Then he took a picture with the Polaroid. "Answer the question, Vernon," he said, pulling the photo out of the camera. "I bet this is going to be one ugly-ass picture. Who is *them*, Vernon?"

Vernon looked at Coach. "The people you're saying are scared of me."

Coach said, "I'll pass. I don't see anyone being scared of your punk ass myself."

"What's wrong with you, man?" Vernon muttered.

"I need answers. That's what's wrong with me. People say they are scared of you, and I don't see why. I asked you if you like to beat up old women or know of anyone who does, and you're not telling me shit."

"No, okay. No, I don't know about any of that."

"Well, tell me about robbing people inside that trashy check-cashing house."

"What?"

"Tell me about it. How many you rob?"

"I didn't rob anybody. I was in that place to see how much it would cost to get a check cashed."

Coach said, "You didn't have a check on you, Vernon."

"I was asking how much it would cost me because I was going to get a check. Ask the man that works in there. He'll tell you. I never robbed anybody, and you don't have any proof that I did, so let me outta here."

"I can tell you this, Vernon. You won't be getting out of here anytime soon."

Vernon said, "Lawyer, then. I want to call a lawyer."

40

By ten o'clock the next morning, Vernon was out of his jail cell and back on the streets with his boys. Coach knew he was out because the watch commander called him and let him know while he was on his way to the hospital to see Lois. He had the Polaroids with him showing ten different angles of this wet wipe Vernon. Unfortunately, when Coach presented them to Lois, she couldn't identify him. Not his face, not his hands, not his arms, not his height, nothing. That would do no good in a court of law, and that was why Vernon's lawyer walked inside and walked out within fifteen minutes. No evidence. Coach went by the check-cashing dump, and to his surprise, there was an out of business sign plastered on the front door and Harry had disconnected his cell phone number and his record of address led to an abandoned house.

The more Coach thought about it, the more he was certain that Vernon and his boys were his prime suspects. They were the only ones making noise in the street at the time. Coach decided all the other stuff concerning the check-cashing scheme was irrelevant and moved it to the back burner for the moment, considering what had happened to Lois. Vernon had stood tall under the pressure from the police, but maybe his boys would not handle the pressure of being yanked and placed in a cell. Coach decided to pay them a visit, but he'd have to find them first.

When Coach saw the Impala for the second time, he wrote down the license plate number, but then he forgot where he had placed the piece of paper. He'd always had a very bad habit of writing things down and not remembering where he wrote them. Even in school he would take notes and place them in a notebook, but then he would have to waste way too much time figuring out exactly where he put them. Coach considered the time it took to look for the license plate number as the cost of doing business, and when he finally found it in the glove compartment of the car, he ran the plate and had a good address for Chucky Lang, the owner of the black Impala.

Chucky Lang was not like his partner in crime Vernon. Along with finding his address, Coach was able to do a background check on Chucky. He found out that he had some sense, at least on paper. He was twenty-two years old and a graduate of Georgia Tech, where he majored in bio-engineering, born and raised in Cobb County, Georgia. His address led Coach to an apartment complex that looked to have three to four hundred units stacked on top of one another, with a clubhouse made of stone in the middle of the complex. Coach parked his Chevy in parking space 331 and sat there for about twenty minutes before he decided to change it up. As he sat outside of Chucky's place, he wondered how a college grad from a top university could end up running the streets with an asshole like Vernon Wise.

There were too many units in the apartment complex and too many cars entering and leaving the parking lot for Coach to even begin looking for a black Impala. So he decided to walk up to the apartment listed on his background check—number 642. Right before he got out of the car, he looked up and was startled to find a black male standing in front of his car, close to the bumper, looking zoned out as he stared into it, trying to see what or who was inside. Coach wasted no time putting his hand on his Glock. From inside the car Coach demanded that the man step back.

The black man didn't move, and Coach thought that maybe the sight of the Glock pointed right at him would make him change his mind. Coach kept aiming the gun at him and opened his door. He stepped out to get a better look at this fool who had been staring into his car like a zombie on crack. Coach kept his distance but still pointed his weapon at the man.

Coach said, "Step up to the car and put your hands on it."

The man began to move.

Coach said, "Nice and slow, gotdamn it."

The man took one step before he was able to put his hands on the car.

Coach said, "So, this is where I ask you, why in the hell are you staring into my car?"

The man chuckled, then said, "He told me you thought you were the shit."

Coach still had his pistol aimed at the man. By now a few bystanders had gathered nearby, and others had stopped their cars. One or two had even started to record the scene with their phones.

Coach said, "What? What are you talking about?"

He said, "Vernon. Vernon, told me your bark is louder than your bite."

"Vernon?"

"Yes, my brother. I'm Chucky Lang."

Coach and Chucky had a few words without moving an inch. Chucky said he fully understood why Coach was there to see him. He said that he wasn't going to talk to him there in the parking lot, though. Said if he wanted any information from him, they should discuss things at a car wash on the other side of town in an hour. Coach was willing to do this because something about this Chucky kid was different. There was no back talk after their first back-and-forth, and he carried himself like a young man growing into manhood. Even so, Coach called for undercover backup at the car wash, which was located thirty minutes away in Smyrna.

When Coach arrived at the car wash, he spotted the black Impala right away on the hand car wash side. It was dripping wet, and Chucky stood on the passenger's side with a towel, wiping it down. Coach pulled up behind him, leaving enough room between them so as not to look suspicious.

"Aren't you going to wash that thing?" Chucky asked when Coach stepped out of the car.

Coach turned and looked at his car. "It's brand new. Barely any dirt on it."

"Not going to look good, sitting here dirty like that while I wipe this down. You can tell that's a cop car a mile away. Why don't you pop the hood or something? Act like you're checking the oil or something?"

Coach was slowly becoming agitated by this guy's stealth tactics but did what he'd asked, anyway, just so he'd shut the hell up and they could get on with it. "So, you bring me way out here. You must have something to tell me." Coach looked across the street and could see the undercovers he'd dispatched watching his every move.

"You're right. I do." Chucky twisted his towel until the water escaped; then he shook it out to normal size and started on the passenger door.

"I'm listening," Coach said.

"He did it." Chucky kept wiping, as if he was getting his car ready for a date.

Coach said, "Say what?" Coach was listening intently to Chucky now.

"Vernon beat her."

"How do you know?"

"I picked him up afterward, him and one of his boys around the corner from the house, and they were laughing about it."

"You actually heard him say that he did it?"

Chucky stopped what he was doing for a brief second. "Of course I'm sure. You think I want to tell on my brother? Well, my stepbrother, but, shit, I've known him all my life."

Coach said, "Tell me what he said in the car when you picked him up."

Chucky was close to getting back to work on his car. "Said there's no way that bitch ain't dead. His exact words."

Coach was silent.

"Yeah, makes you mad, don't it? But this is my first and last time telling someone about this. No more police, no court, none of that shit."

Coach looked at him.

He said, "I'm serious, man. I will never admit to telling you any of this."

"Well, why are you doing it now?"

"Because it needs doin'. Look, I'm a college grad, man. It has taken me damn near a year to find a job. My career choice is one of the most coveted in the nation, and here I am, stuck in this bitch, and couldn't even find work until last week, and the job's out west."

Coach didn't really know where he was going with this.

"You want to know why?" Chucky walked to his trunk and pulled out a dry towel. He held it up to show Coach when he saw him position his hand to grab his Glock quickly if the need arose.

"It's cool," Coach said. "So tell me."

Chucky went back to work on his car. "'Cause of people like Vernon, that's why. All the shit he does, and people like him, on a daily basis. It makes people take it out on every black male that looks like him in every aspect of life. Like out in the country . . . hell, to a farmer a fox look like a fox, right?"

Coach said, "I guess."

"Guess, your ass. I don't even blame people for their fucked-up stereotypes anymore. Not even when they read all my credentials and my shit is one hundred percent better than anyone else's. So that's why I'm telling you, Detective, so you can find a way to put his black ass in jail."

Coach said, "Well, how am I supposed to do that when you won't back up what you say?"

Chucky said, "Not my problem. But I'll tell you this. Vernon has been stockpiling weapons for the past year. Don't ask me where, 'cause I don't know."

Coach said, "You're still not telling me a damn thing where I can get him off the street."

Chucky stalled for a beat. He lifted up one of his windshield wiper blades. "Well, you know the guy that I told you I picked up with Vernon the night the lady was beat up?"

"Yeah. I'm listening."

"He's dead. His body is laying up in that check-cashing spot where you snatched up Vernon."

41

After the powwow with Chucky Lang, Coach called for a cruiser by radio to head over to the check-cashing shop, and within minutes they were standing in the middle of a murder scene.

When Coach got there, he was told that the deceased, Mark Hollow, was a well-known street criminal who had been in the system since his teenage years. There was not much to do there besides check for fingerprints, as they decided that Mark had been murdered at another location and his body had then been placed inside the shop. Chucky Lang's tip had paid off, and it was too bad that Coach couldn't tap his resource any longer, because Chucky was on the road, heading out west, never to return.

Coach knew that they had to bring Vernon back in. From the time he left the police station they had had a tail on him and knew his whereabouts. Right now officers were sitting directly in front of his home. This Vernon was smart, and more than likely he had made a call to have Mark Hollow killed, otherwise, the tail would have followed him to the murder scene. Coach even thought that just maybe Chucky did the deed. He put that thought back in his mental file. For some reason, he was cheering for Chucky, wanted him to succeed and make something of his life.

Coach would have to work from home for a couple of hours, though. It was Shonda's birthday, and she wanted to have a small, quiet dinner with just the two men in her life, along with Calvin and her girlfriend Sherri, who she thought might be a good fit for Calvin. He had continually nagged Shonda for an invite and a friend introduction after seeing Sherri at their last game.

"J, you really look good in that suit, my man," Calvin said. They had just finished dinner, and Coach was placing the birthday cake on the table. It was a double chocolate cake that he had ordered for Shonda at the neighborhood bakery.

Jarques didn't acknowledge Calvin other than giving him a head nod. He proceeded to pass the dessert plates around the table. When Coach sat back down, Jarques began to listen to what the Coach had to say.

Coach looked around the table. *Wow. A family moment,* he thought. "This is really special because it's the first birthday we have spent together," Coach said. "And I really hope we can share more of your birthdays together, Shonda." He looked around the table. "So, saying that, I think this would be a good time to go around the table and let Shonda know how much she means to us on her birthday."

Shonda placed a smile on her face. "No, you don't have to do that."

"Oh yes, we do," Calvin said, pushing. "I am very happy to know you right about now, and you too, Sherri." Calvin moved his chair closer to Sherri.

"See? There you go, Calvin," Shonda pointed out.

Sherri was not shy. She stepped right in and shared with the others how Shonda had always been there for her and how much she enjoyed working with her on a daily basis. When she finished talking, she even stood up, walked around the table, and gave Shonda a big hug.

When she sat back down, Calvin moved even closer to Sherri.

Then it was Jarques's turn, and he looked at all the smiling people around the table, waiting to hear what he had to say. "I love you, Mom, but I wish you would get rid of his ass," he blurted as he pointed at Coach.

Calvin had really moved in on Sherri at this point and was so mesmerized by her that he told Jarques, "Nice job." When he suddenly realized what Jarques had said, he looked up and said, "Huh? Say what?"

There was a brief silence, because no one believed what had just come out of Jarques's mouth. Coach was stunned that Jarques had said this about him.

Jarques shouted, "I don't like him, he shouldn't be here, and I want him to stop coming over here."

There was no mistaking what he was saying now.

"Jarques, what's your problem? You better apologize right now." Shonda ordered.

"No." Jarques got up from the table and walked out of the kitchen, through the living room, and out the front door.

Everyone at the table was dumbfounded and couldn't imagine what was happening. Calvin stood up to go after Jarques, but Coach interceded and let him know that he'd go see what was going on. Shonda didn't move, because she was trying to understand it all.

Jarques was standing on the small concrete porch just outside the house. When he noticed Coach standing at the door, peering at him, he stepped off the porch, headed down the driveway to the sidewalk, and stood right under a street lamp.

Jarques looked back and noticed Coach was walking up on him. "You still here?"

Coach was very confused as to what was going on. "Yeah, I'm here," he said quietly.

"Well, why don't you leave?"

Coach stopped and stood behind Jarques. "Look, did I miss something here? Did I do something?"

"Yes, man, I already told you. You're here."

Coach looked up at the street lamp and took a deep breath. "Look, why don't you turn around like a man and talk to me?"

Jarques didn't move. "The same reason you didn't tell me that being seen with you was going to get me killed."

Coach was taken aback by his words. He tried to understand what he was saying. "What do you mean, get you killed?" Coach walked around to face Jarques, and then Jarques turned his back on him again. "Damn it, son, talk to me."

"I'm not your son," Jarques remarked.

Coach opened his arms, then dropped them to his sides. "Jarques, what are you talking about, get you killed?"

Coach stood there without saying another word until Jarques got that he was not leaving until he found out what he was talking about.

Jarques said, "I'm talking about at school."

"At school?"

"All day today there was a crew of boys that kept coming up to me, saying things, handing me notes."

"Saying what? What kind of notes?"

"Telling me, 'Tell your daddy cop to back off, and if your daddy don't back off, we know where you and your mother live.'" Jarques finally looked Coach in the eye. He screamed, "Do you know how it is to move around school like that? Do you know how it feels to be threatened all day, and you don't even know what it's about? I couldn't even tell my mother, because I didn't want her to know."

"Tell me what, Jarques?" Shonda said. She had come out of the house. As she headed their way, Coach knew he would have to explain. "What? What is it, Jarques?"

Jarques didn't answer. He looked at Coach.

"There are some boys at school that are threatening him," Coach said.

"Threatening? About what?" She went to put her arm around Jarques, but he moved away from her.

"The case that I'm working on. I guess they have seen me drop him off at school or something," Coach explained.

All sorts of thoughts were running through Shonda's mind at lightning speed. "What?"

Coach tried to put his arm around Shonda. "You don't have to worry. I'll—"

"Jarques, are you okay?" Shonda said.

The boy nodded his head yes.

"Go inside. I need to talk to Coach for a second."

Coach began to pace a bit, thinking about that fool Vernon, who had found a way to get at Jarques. He said, "Look, Shonda—"

She cut him off. "No, you look. That's my boy in there. I don't know what kind of case you're working on that now involves my son, but this is not going to work."

"Shonda, listen . . . I will get to the bottom of this. Jarques will be fine," Coach said.

She said, "How do you know that? How the hell, all of a sudden, can my son be brought into something you're doing on your job? Do you even know what he's talking about?"

Coach hesitated and put his head down. "Murder."

She moved closer to him. "What did you say?"

"Shonda, it's a murder case."

Shonda almost screamed but covered her mouth. "Murder?"

"Yes."

She began to cry. "Good-bye, Coach."

Coach tried to move close to her.

"Good-bye," she repeated, then turned and walked away.

42

Within two minutes Coach was in the car with Calvin, and the only sound that could be heard was the new tires on the Chevy making love to the pavement.

"You mind telling me where we going?" Calvin said. "Shoot, man, I had something working back there. I didn't even get a chance to get her number."

"Got to go. Some personal business I need to take care of," Coach said.

Calvin said, "What do you think I was trying to do back there?"

Coach didn't respond.

"What's the problem, man? What the hell happened back there with Jarques, and why are you driving like we are chasing somebody?"

"Damn case I'm on. A crew at Jarques's school threatened him, and he's mad at me. I know who is behind it, though."

"Threat? Like the threat against Lois?"

"Yeah, against him and his mother."

"So where you going?"

"To handle this."

"You're going to drop me off first, right?"

"Sorry. You gotta roll with me."

"Oh, no, the hell I don't," Calvin said. "See? What did I tell you? You mess with the team mom, and there's nothing but problems. I guess every man has to learn on his own."

"That's all unrelated. This guy I have been chasing has had this whole side of town on edge. Has people doing shit for him because he gives them no choice. Not going to happen here, though."

Calvin said, "So, you know where he lives?"

"Yeah, I've had a tail on him since he left the police station when we couldn't get a charge to stick."

"So you're calling for backup, right?"

Coach held up his Glock. "This is my backup."

Calvin responded by moving closer to his car door.

"There is an unmarked car in front of his house, so we're good," Coach said.

"I know you don't expect me to go up in there with you. Shit, I'm not a cop."

"Stay in the car, Calvin. Can you do that?"

"You don't have to ask, believe that."

Coach pushed on the gas pedal, and the car took off like a plane on the runway. Calvin reached for his seat belt and strapped in nice and tight.

Before long Coach pulled up to the address where they had the tail on Vernon. Coach quickly explained to the officer on surveillance that he needed to go in and get Vernon. Calvin could see everything going on, and he slid down into his seat, just in case bullets began to fly.

Coach yelled, "Police!" only one time before he kicked the door, his Glock in his hand and a bulletproof vest covering his chest. When the door burst open, he and the officer on surveillance rushed inside. They were inside for only five or six minutes before they came back out. They had a few heated words back and forth, and then Coach plopped back down in the front seat of the car and slammed the door shut.

Coach was silent. He was breathing heavily.

"You all right, man?" Calvin said.

"He's not there. How in the hell is he not there?"

For the next five minutes or so, on the way to taking Calvin home, Coach remained completely silent.

Calvin said, "So that's probably it between you two, huh?"

Coach turned to look at him. "Told me good-bye."

"Damn," Calvin acknowledged.

"Thought I was getting back into it the right way, man."

"Well, that's how things work out. When you think you're doing the right thing, something always comes a-knocking, and nothing you can do but deal with it."

"She's probably scared out of her mind right about now, getting threats like that," Coach said.

"So, what're you going to do?"

"I got to find this guy. Make sure they are okay in the meantime."

Coach pulled up to Calvin's place.

"Hey, be safe out here, Coach."

"Yeah, thanks."

Who would have thought that Coach would be told that it was over between him and Shonda and that the guy he had been chasing had fucked up his relationship and scared the hell out of Shonda and Jarques at the same time? Coach didn't have too many options at this point other than to find this guy and have him locked up. There was no way he was going to have anyone testify against him in a court of law, because Lois didn't see his face, his brother was long gone by now, having headed out west to his new job, and the cavernous asshole who had witnessed the beating and thought Vernon was a friend was in the morgue.

Coach was not going out like this. This was his very first case and his only case at the moment, and he was going to have to take responsibility for going awkwardly in the wrong direction. He didn't know which way to go, but for now, he was on his way back to keep an eye on Shonda and Jarques, even though he would have to do it from inside his car.

Coach parked his car right in front of Shonda's place and didn't care who saw it there. He was determined not to let anything happen to them. Losing two women whom he cared about would be too much for any man to bear. About three hours passed, and it was close to one in the morning when his cell phone rang as he was about to doze off.

He answered, "Yeah."

The watch commander said, "Just got a call at the front desk."

"Yeah? From who?"

The watch commander seemed as though he had been in a deep sleep. "Lois Gregory's address."

Coach sat all the way up. "Yeah? What about it?"

"Get over there. There's something you might want to see."

Coach didn't want to leave Shonda's house unguarded, so he called in a cruiser and told the officer to sit tight until he returned. He sped over to Lois's to see what was so pressing. When he arrived there, he found at least six police cars, all with flashing lights, and yellow tape surrounding the house. When Coach walked inside, he almost became deflated when he saw the body of Chucky Lang, who was supposed to be on his way out west to start his new job.

43

Just like the body in the check-cashing joint, Chucky Lang's body had been put in the house after he was shot somewhere else. His opportunity out west was not going to happen. Coach knew that Vernon was sending him a message and cleaning up his mess by shooting both Chucky and Mark twice in the head. Coach didn't know what Vernon would do next, so he stationed himself back in front of Shonda's house before they placed Chucky Lang's body on ice, to make sure she and Jarques would be safe.

Coach had to call Lois and Mr. Tall at the hospital to let them know what had taken place and even though it was sad for Lois, Coach was relieved to find out that Mr. Tall would be at the hospital, watching over her, and they would be somewhat safe there.

Shonda was aware that Coach had sat in front of her home most of the night. She couldn't sleep, and for most of the night, she looked out her blinds at him. When she came outside early the next morning and tapped on his window, he gave her a half smile, still feeling sorry for what her family was going through. He rolled down the window.

"Want some coffee?" she said.

His smile told her yes, and she handed a cup to him.

"So, are you going to invite me in?" she said.

"Yeah, sure, c'mon."

Coach kept his eyes on Shonda the entire time she maneuvered around his car to the passenger's side in her housecoat and slippers. When she got inside the car, she wrapped her arms around her chest and burrowed her hands deep into her housecoat.

"Wow, it is chilly out here," she said.

Coach transferred the coffee from one hand to another so he could start up the car. "The heat in here will get you right." He sipped his coffee and smiled. "Thanks."

"Least I can do, since you have been out here all night," she said.

"Look, I'm sorry. I never knew my case would have long enough legs to involve you and Jarques. I should have never taken him to school or told the perp that I am investigating that I remembered him from the park. He's probably been following me without me even knowing it."

She took a deep breath. "It's okay, Coach. How were you supposed to know? I've been thinking about it. You can't control anyone but yourself, and you have treated me and my son very nice, and I appreciate it."

"Thank you," Coach told her, then drank more java.

"I didn't sleep one wink last night," she confessed.

"Really?"

"Nope. I was thinking about you . . . about us. I decided that you can't run scared in life. No matter what it brings you, you cannot run scared."

"And you don't have to be afraid, because I will be here every night until I lock this bastard up. I promise you that," Coach said.

Shonda gathered her thoughts before she spoke. "So, what do you do next? How are you going to get this guy?"

Coach didn't have an answer right off.

"I just don't want Jarques to have to worry. He still has to go to school and to other activities," Shonda told him.

"Well, if they are watching him, it probably would be best if they saw him ride with me."

She grabbed on to Coach's hand. "I think so too."

"I will call the school resource officer and make sure he has Jarques in his sight all day long, and I'll station an undercover car right outside the school."

"Okay, good," Shonda agreed. "So, you'll come inside for some breakfast and promise to stay with me tonight?"

He smiled. "Yes, and every night, if you guys will have me."

During breakfast Shonda explained to Jarques that she thought it would be a good idea for him to be seen with police protection to prevent anything from happening to him. Jarques was not in a very receptive mood, but he hated to see his mom in such a worried state, and so he agreed.

After breakfast Coach and Jarques headed to school. They were quiet in the car. Coach didn't want to say anything that would upset Jarques. On the other hand, the kid was kind of embarrassed about going off the way he had, understanding now that he could have just come out and told the adults what was going on. The police radio was the only sound in the car as it blasted directions to locations of early morning accidents and a few domestic disputes.

Coach turned to him. "Jarques, look, I want to apologize for getting you upset due to my work."

Jarques was still listening to the car radio. "So, all this stuff is just happening minute by minute?"

"Huh?"

"On this radio. Things happen so fast."

"Oh, yeah, that's the way it happens," Coach assured him.

"So the cops handle that, and you handle the investigation?"

"Right . . ."

Jarques continued to listen to the radio.

"Jarques, did you hear me apologize?" Coach said.

"Yeah, I heard you."

"I mean it. I should have been more aware."

"It's not your fault. How could you know?"

Coach thought about what he had said. "Yeah, but it's my job to know. It's my job."

There was another few minutes of silence.

"So, think you'll be able to trust me now?" Coach asked him.

Jarques thought about it. "Yeah, I think so."

Coach said, "My man."

They gave one another a pound with their fists.

"Well, you know what they say. In order for two people to trust each other, they really have to know one another."

Jarques turned to look at him. "What's that supposed to mean?"

"It means that I am going to tell you something that I haven't even told your mom yet, and you have to promise me you won't tell anyone."

He smiled. "What? You got kids somewhere? You married, Coach? Maybe a woman on the other side of town?" Jarques loved his own jokes.

"No, boy."

"What then?"

"You really want to know?"

"You're the one who offered, and if you're going to tell me, you better hurry up, because school is right up the street. . . ."

"I'm a millionaire."

Jarques paused and let what Coach had said to him soak in, and then he began to laugh. The thought of Coach being a millionaire got so good to him that he couldn't stop laughing.

Coach turned and looked at him after he stopped the car in front of the school. "What?

What's wrong?"

Jarques grabbed his books and opened the car door. "Okay, trust me, Coach, I'll never tell anyone. A millionaire, right . . ." Then he got out of the car and walked away.

44

The watch commander was not in a brother-in-law-loving mood, as he was being pushed by higher-ups for answers concerning the connected murders. He wanted to see Coach as soon as possible and called a meeting with him without delay in order to understand what the hell was going on, because things had gotten out of hand. When Coach walked toward his door, the watch commander waved him into his office without wasting any time.

"How many more, Coach? How many more?"

Coach replied, "He's cleaning up his past. That's all I can say. Everyone connected to him has been killed, so that they can't testify against any of the shit he's done."

"So, you're telling me that he's smarter than you?"

"What?"

"You're the one who is supposed to find witnesses and get people to testify, and everybody that you know that can do just that ends up getting killed."

"He's thought this out. This guy thinks about what he is doing way before he does it and picks out people he knows he can get next to and control."

"Well, this guy needs to get picked up. I don't know how you're going to do it, but it needs to be done. As a matter of fact, you can start with a press conference in an hour."

"Whoa. Say what?"

"Aren't you still the public relations officer in this unit?"

"Well, yeah, but you were supposed to find someone else for that."

"But I haven't, so change your clothes and do what you do best, because I'm tired of trying to answer all these gotdamned reporters."

"I have to get back on the streets," Coach said.

The watch commander said, "Afterward. It shouldn't be that hard. You're the lead investigator, so just tell them what you just told me."

Being ambushed by the watch commander was nothing new for Coach, so he went down to the locker room and put on his day uniform, which he'd worn whenever he needed to address the press before he became a detective. While getting dressed, he thought about all the possible questions that might come from the four or five reporters who usually peppered him with questions. Coach had to play his cards right. There was no way he was going to tell them that he was the lead detective on the case. He promised himself to stay away from any questions that would lead the reporters to asking who the lead detective was.

He was downstairs in the briefing room exactly at eleven, and the reporters were there, awaiting his arrival. There were way more than four or five reporters waiting to find out what was going on, and they didn't waste any time.

"We understand there has been a beating of a senior citizen and two murders in the last few weeks and they are all connected. Is that correct?" one reporter said. He didn't have a notepad. He just shoved his recorder in Coach's face and waited for his answer.

"Yes, that's correct. There has been an assault and two murders. We are still working on establishing whether they are connected or not."

"How will you determine if they are connected or not?" Another reporter asked. She was a reporter from the small community newspaper that always did a much better job than any major paper ever could.

Coach said, "The department will put the pieces of the puzzle together, like we always have, and will determine if they are connected."

"Do you have a suspect?" asked another reporter.

Coach thought for a moment. In his position as a public relations officer, he had never given a suspect's name. It wasn't the department's policy, for some reason or another. But he was a detective now. And he needed to get this bastard.

"Yes, yes, we do. As a matter of fact, we had him in for questioning, but our victim was unable to identify him and we had to let him back out on the streets," Coach said.

"You mean to tell us, you let a killer walk right out the door of this building?" said one of the reporters.

"Well, at that time he wasn't a killer. But now this is what we know. A family member of this suspect reported to us that he was involved. But now that witness is dead. We also suspect that he has killed everyone who could place him at the scene of the assault of the senior citizen. Everyone, from his friends to even his own family member."

"Do you have a name?"

"A name?" Coach repeated. "Yes, his name is Vernon. Vernon Wise. And here is a picture of him as well."

After the question-and-answer session was finished, Coach was happy with the progress he'd made, because if Vernon wanted to play hide-and-seek, now he had to hide from more than one person. In fact, he had to hide from the entire city, if he was still here.

45

For Harry, it seemed as though life had been hell ever since he closed his check-cashing operation. It was a business that he'd owned for the past sixteen years, and he had never planned on doing anything else. It wasn't his fault it was closed. Vernon had made him close it, and then Vernon had been bold enough to move into his home and take control of everything inside, including his daughters and anything else that he wanted. Harry's home was large enough for everyone to spread out and not be on top of one another. It was great for Harry and his two daughters. But when Vernon decided that this was the place where he was going to put his next crime in motion, his presence was felt in every corner of the house, and that made it an awful place to be.

Vernon had Harry move the furniture in their family room so that Vernon would have his back toward the wall and could face anyone who entered the room. The room had a couch, a television, some chairs, and a few small tables. On this day Vernon was sitting on the couch, peering at Harry's daughters. One was seventeen, and the other was maybe nine. There were several pistols lying next to Vernon on the couch, and a few assault rifles lay on the floor by his feet.

"Come here, Harry," Vernon said.

Harry's daughters looked over at their father, then back at Vernon, wondering what he wanted this time, as Harry did as he was told. Harry tried to give his daughters the most calming smile he could muster to sooth their nerves, but it didn't work. When he got close enough to Vernon, he stopped without saying a word, and it was apparent that he was mortified by Vernon and everything he was about.

Vernon said, "How long have I known you?"

Harry didn't have an exact answer for him, so he didn't reply. He'd been scolded earlier and bitch slapped in front of his daughters for not knowing exactly how many beers were in the fridge.

Vernon said, "Here we go. Are we going to play that fuckin' game today, Harry? Gotdamn it, when I ask you a question, just answer it, okay?"

"I'll try," Harry mumbled. "About three months," he said.

Vernon smiled. "Wrong."

"No?" Harry said.

"Hell no, it's been three months and six days. Damn it, man. Don't you remember anything?"

Harry was about to speak, but Vernon told him to shut the hell up.

"Listen, while you were out getting my beer, I turned on the twelve o'clock news and I watched it with your daughters." He waved over at them with twinkling fingers and a crooked smile. "Don't you want to know what they said about me on the news, Harry?"

Harry nodded yes.

"No, no, gotdamn it. Let's have some interaction, some communication. Fuckin' ask me, man."

Harry looked over at his daughters and they looked away from him. He carefully selected his words before he spoke. "Vernon, can you tell me why you were on the news today?"

Vernon looked at him like a teacher waiting for something.

"Please," Harry said quickly. "Please."

Vernon smiled, then pushed himself back against the couch to sit up straight. "Well, it seems like these motherfuckers think I beat up an old lady and killed two people and put one of the dead bodies in your little broken-down business venture around the way."

Harry remained silent and tried to listen to every word that was said to him.

"I know . . . crazy, huh?" Vernon said. "As long as you've known me, have you ever known me to kill a man, Harry?"

"No, no, I haven't," Harry answered.

"Well, this detective thinks I did. He thinks I did so much that he said my name on television and showed the entire city my picture so people can see me if I go out into the streets. Have you ever been a wanted man, Harry?"

"No, no, I haven't," Harry said.

"Of course you haven't. You haven't done anything wrong, except maybe come over here to this country illegally and change your name to Harry Henry. But never mind that, Harry, because I always say, 'The more the merrier.'" He looked over at the girls. "Right, ladies?"

The girls turned their heads from Vernon, and the oldest put her arm around her little sister because she hadn't stopped shaking since the fool Vernon had taken them all hostage. Harry was becoming very uncomfortable with the looks Vernon had been shooting his daughters, but he knew he was no match for Vernon physically and refused to say a word about it.

"So, Harry, since this guy wants to make my life uncomfortable, guess what? That's going to make your life uncomfortable too. That is why I want you to come over here and choose one of these rifles lying at my feet," Vernon said.

Harry looked down and could see the rifles all at his feet, along with the pistols on the couch.

"Don't make me tell you twice." Vernon's voice was ice cold now.

Harry moved closer to him.

"Go 'head and pick one up," Vernon said.

Harry looked at Vernon, trying to read him, as this might be some sort of trick.

"It's cool, man. I just want you to pick it up," Vernon said.

Harry bent down to grab a rifle as quickly as he could, trying to keep his eyes on Vernon the entire time, while Vernon cheered him on. When Harry finally secured the rifle in his hands, he placed it in firing position and pointed it directly at Vernon's head and pulled the trigger over and over and over again.

Vernon pushed his back against the couch again and again, pretending to be shot, and then had a good laugh at Harry's expense. His voice was higher pitched when he said, "Harry, do you really think I would give your stupid ass a loaded assault weapon at this moment in time? Huh, do you?"

Harry still had the weapon in his hands but was more scared than he had ever been because of what he had attempted to do.

"You should be scared, Harry, but I don't blame you. I have taken over your home, and guess what? If you don't do exactly what I tell you, I'm going to take your daughters too, both of them. So, I understand your anger, and that's going to make what I have for you to do that much easier for you."

Harry didn't respond to the threat, as he was given a full understanding of what Vernon meant when Vernon ordered Harry's oldest daughter to sit on the floor, facing him, without her shirt on so Vernon could lust after her breasts, while he gave Harry instructions on what he wanted done with the assault rifle Harry was still holding in his hands.

46

Days had passed, and the trail to Vernon had turned ice cold. Coach was beginning to think Vernon had left town to terrorize another community and its citizens. Coach was still spending every night with Shonda and Jarques and driving around the community with the rest of officers in his precinct during the day, searching every possible place that Vernon could be. Known criminals on the streets didn't even want to talk about Vernon after finding out that he had done his own brother for talking.

Coach welcomed the end of the football season at the park more than he ever had in the past. This season he actually felt as though he had let his team down, even though they had one game to go and, if they were victorious, would head into the play-offs. Coach would be the first to admit that his current investigation had pulled him away from his team, and he intended to make the last week of practice leading up to the final game a time that the kids would never forget, whether they won or lost on Saturday, because in his eyes they deserved it. All through the week Coach had dinner for the kids catered after practice and gave them five different T-shirts apiece for their wardrobes that would promote the team and the park for years to come.

Calvin, on the other hand, wanted to continue playing in the play-offs, and during the last practice he worked the team as hard as he could, believing that they had the upper hand on their opponent this upcoming weekend.

And if they stuck to the game plan, they would have another week of practice and another game to play. After a round of wind sprints and a water break, the coaches brought the team together in a huddle to begin working on offense. Coach smiled as he watched Shonda gather the water bottles to refill them.

After the coaches set the players up on the defense that their opponent would most likely run this weekend, they began to give the players on offense their blocking assignments one by one to ensure everyone would know what to do come game day. Coach was working with the line on a play, and Calvin was in the backfield, in a player's face about not fumbling in the upcoming game.

As practice continued, Harry watched from afar in his car. He was worn and tired. He couldn't sleep with that animal in the house with his daughters, and now Vernon was there all alone with them. Vernon's promise to leave them be and get out of their lives for good was all that Harry was focusing on as he sat in the front seat with the loaded assault rifle, given to him to turn on the entire football team at the end of practice. Harry had never been so out of his mind before. His lack of sleep had pushed him into doing exactly what Vernon wanted him to do, as had his concern for the well-being of his dear daughters, who lost their mother when they were only babies and needed their father. At this point, he was willing to do whatever was necessary for their safety. No matter what.

Vernon had told Harry to make sure he waited until 7:30 p.m. to turn the weapon on the team. At 7:25 p.m. the cell phone Vernon had given him rang. Harry answered, keeping his eyes on the team members, who looked to be taking off their helmets and gathering in a circle to end practice.

"They should be ending practice by now," Vernon said.

Harry didn't answer.

"Hey, gotdamn it! Did they finish practice or what?"

Harry remained silent until he heard his older daughter scream. "Yes, yes, they are in a circle now," Harry said.

"Well, what are you waiting for? Go out there, point that rifle at them, and just pull the trigger until it stops firing. Then get back here to get your daughters," Vernon said.

Vernon's orders at this point seemed as if they were doable when Harry overheard Vernon ask for another kiss from his daughter. It took Harry over the edge, and he threw the phone on the car floor, picked up the rifle, climbed out from behind the wheel, and walked onto the field.

Dusk had fallen on the field. Harry stood about thirty yards from the team and tried to place the rifle in the same position Vernon had shown him at the house, because he was told that it would be hard to handle the rifle otherwise. Harry had never fired a semiautomatic rifle before. Or any rifle, for that matter, except for the BB gun he had had for a month or two as a child, before his mother took it away from him. Harry asked God to forgive him before he lifted the rifle one last time.

As Calvin and Coach addressed their team amid the falling darkness, Calvin looked up and could not believe what he was seeing. Calvin tapped Coach on the arm, and Coach did not have to think twice about what was about to go down. Coach tried to collect himself.

"Guys," Coach said to his team, "I want everybody to gather in real tight for me. Don't look back. Just do what the hell I say right now." As the team gathered closer together, Coach told them to put their helmets on and, when he told them to run, to run as fast as they could across to the other side of the field. But before he could tell them to run, he noticed Shonda walk in front of the gunman and called out her name. Now Shonda and Harry were standing face-to-face, and Shonda was not blinking an eye.

"Move out the way, lady. Are you crazy?"

"She paused. "Maybe I am."

Who are you, lady?"

"I'm the team mom."

Standing with his teammates, Jarques turned around and saw his mother, and began to run toward her, but Calvin grabbed him by the arm and struggled to keep him from bolting. Coach started walking in Shonda's direction and called out several times for the man to put down his weapon.

Harry repeated, "I said, 'Move out of the way,'"

"No, I will not move," Shonda said. She looked back at Jarques when he called out her name.

"I mean it, lady! Move right now, or I will shoot you first!"

"Well, go 'head and do it, damn it, because you're not shooting those boys!"

Harry tried to sidestep Shonda, but she continued to move in front of him and the rifle. "I have to do this. Get the fuck out of the way!" he said.

"You *have* to do it? Why would you have to harm these boys?"

"He told me too. I have to, or he's going to kill my daughters."

Harry tried to sidestep Shonda again, and she moved in his line of fire again.

"Will you please move, gotdamn it! Please . . . If I don't do this, my daughters are dead."

"Sir, look, I don't know what's going on right now. But I do know that I am *not* moving, and if you want to shoot them, you have to start with me."

Harry was getting annoyed and took the rifle and aimed it right at Shonda's head. "Okay, if this is how you want it," he said.

Jarques screamed out for his mother. Shonda looked Harry right in the eye while they stood in the same position for what seemed like hours. Harry began to cry and moved his finger on the trigger, then yanked the rifle down and fell to his knees and wept. Seconds later Coach and Calvin grabbed him and took the rifle away.

47

Everyone on the field was saying their prayers, and parents were running onto the field, clutching their sons and wanting to kick the shit out of Harry, even though he had put the rifle down. Coach called in cruisers, and when they arrived, officers placed Harry in the back of one of the cruisers. Coach climbed in next to Harry. He had no time for any games.

"You remember me, Harry?" Coach said.

For the first time Harry looked up and focused in on Coach. His eyes were red from crying. "Yeah, you're that detective guy."

"That's right. I'm only going to ask you this one time, Harry, before they go and lock your ass up and you never see the crack of daylight again. What the fuck, Harry? What the fuck is this all about, man?"

Harry had his hands cuffed behind his back. "He's going to kill my daughters," he said. "He's probably done it by now."

"Who is he?" Coach asked.

"The fucking asshole who took my place of business hostage. He's in my house with my daughters. Told me if I didn't come down here and shoot up the team, he was going to kill them."

"Vernon?"

"Yes. By now, I'm sure, he has already hurt them."

Finally, a break on where the asshole had been hiding out. Coach could feel the adrenaline pumping through his body because he was pissed. Pissed that Shonda had to be taken to the hospital to be treated for shock, pissed that this fuckin' asshole didn't have enough balls not to give in to Vernon's threat to hurt his daughters at the expense of others, and pissed at Vernon for taking advantage and terrorizing so many people.

Within minutes they had a tactical squad in front of Harry's home, and the first thing that they did was cut off all power to the house. Coach had Harry placed in his car, and after he got all the information from Harry about his daughters' and Vernon's exact location in the home, Coach relayed it to the SWAT team. They had made up their minds that there would be no negotiations when they arrived on the scene. They were going to burst through the house and take this asshole dead or alive.

All Coach could do now as he stood beside his Chevy was wait and see as the SWAT team went to work. Harry stood beside him in cuffs as the SWAT team announced themselves and went inside. A couple minutes later Harry saw his daughters running out of the house and screamed out their names. Coach took off Harry's cuffs before he was reunited with his daughters, and then patted him on the back, because he truly understood family. A few minutes later, Vernon was led out by officers, hands cuffed behind his back, and within minutes he was on his way to jail for the rest of his sad life.

48

It had never been done before. For the very first time the team wanted to have their banquet on the practice field, in celebration of what could have been. On the day of the banquet parents pitched in, setting up tables on the field, helping organize the catered food, and lining up all the players' trophies on a table for all to see. Even though the team didn't make the play-offs, they thought this day was very special. It was a day to celebrate life.

Mr. Tall was there, along with Lois, and they were relieved that the nightmare in the community had come to an end. Calvin had finally been able to catch up with Shonda's friend Sherri and had invited her as his date. Shonda and Coach were enjoying themselves too, as *this* chapter in their lives had ended on very good terms.

ORDER FORM
URBAN BOOKS, LLC
97 N18th Street
Wyandanch, NY 11798

Name (please print):_____

Address: _____

City/State: _____

Zip: _____

QTY	TITLES	PRICE

Shipping and handling: add $3.50 for 1st book, then $1.75 for each additional book.

Please send a check payable to:

Urban Books, LLC

Please allow 4-6 weeks for delivery